The

MISADVENTURES OF
Catie Bloom

BROOKE STANTON

COCO
— *and bee* —

The Misadventures of Catie Bloom by Brooke Stanton

Copyright © 2016 by Brooke Chirone. All rights reserved.

Cover Art by Daliborka Mijailovic

ISBN: 0996851402
ISBN-13: 978-0-9968514-0-4

FOR MICK

Chapter 1

CATIE

B linking from the bright studio lights, I scan my notes. "Do you need any water?" Karen, the executive producer, calls out from the darkness.

"I'm fine."

Mandy from hair and makeup comes at me with a powder brush. Looking me over, she pulls my dark hair in front of my shoulders and smooths it down.

"Don't touch," she gently scolds. Last month, I ran my fingers through my hair, and my oversized turquoise ring got stuck in my tresses, forcing me to do the whole segment with my hand cupping the right side of my head.

There's a scurry of movement as Holly Jenkins, the co-host of *Wake Up, America!*, leaves the living room set and joins me in the kitchen set, where I'm standing behind the counter. After reviewing her note cards, Holly looks at the prepped ingredients in front of us: sliced beets and onions, walnuts, arugula, goat cheese, a halved orange, honey, and a caddy with extra-virgin olive oil, salt, and pepper.

"Back in three," Karen says, emerging from the darkness beyond the lights and pulling Holly aside for a quick chat.

Squinting, I look beyond the cameras for my sister, Natalie. I know this is an easy recipe—only a salad—but without Natalie nearby, my anxiety is rising.

Holly is back by my side as the red light of camera two flicks on. I look frantically around the studio. *Where the hell is Natalie?*

"Welcome back," Holly says to the camera, her hair, makeup, and couture perfect. "Joining me in the kitchen today is Catelyn Bloom from *Simply Chic* magazine. She's going to show us the trick to making a gourmet salad in under ten minutes." Holly turns her dazzling smile to me.

"Right, uh…" I glance at my cards. I've done these cooking segments on *Wake Up, America!* a half-dozen times, but always with Natalie in my line of vision, coaching me along. "Today we're making a goat cheese and roasted-beet salad."

"Looks delicious." Holly beams. "But there are a lot of ingredients laid out. How do you do it all in under ten minutes? What's the trick?"

"It's easier than you think. First…"

Oh, God! What's the trick?

Just then, Natalie's face appears to the right of the camera. She motions to the beets.

Oh, right—beets.

"Instead of buying fresh beets, which you have to boil for ages, and a whole onion, which you have to peel and cut, buy presliced onions and canned beets, available in most supermarkets. Then all you have to do is place them in a roasting pan"—which I do—"drizzle with olive oil and salt and pepper, and stick them in the oven at 350 for 10 minutes."

"It's so simple!" Holly's eyes widen as if I've just given her the cure for cancer.

"While that's roasting, whisk the honey, oil, and juice of one orange together in a bowl." Reaching into the refrigerator, I pull out a plate of already-cooked beets and onions. "And when the beets and onions are done roasting, scoop them into a salad bowl with the arugula and walnuts, and add the dressing mixture. Voilà! The salad is—"

From the corner of my eye, I see Natalie waving her hands and pointing wildly. I snap a glance at her and follow her finger.

"Erm…I mean, don't forget the star ingredient: goat cheese! Crumble it on top, and there you are. A gourmet salad in under ten minutes."

"As always, delicious and so easy." Holly takes a tiny bite with her fork and washes it down with water. "Your husband is one lucky man."

I cringe at her words and don't dare look at Natalie.

"You'll find the full recipe at our website, WakeUp.com" Holly takes another drink of water. Her skin glows in the bright lights. "We're going to head over to Ed Priestly for the weather report. Then we'll be back with more from *Simply Chic*'s Catelyn Bloom."

Holly holds her smile and then relaxes as the red light goes off. Karen snatches her, and I hear Holly ask, "How many calories are in beets? I can only have twelve hundred…" Her voice trails off, and I mouth *thank you* to Natalie as I quickly look over my notes for the next segment, "Husband Emergency: How to Handle a Bad Gift Giver."

***

An hour later, I'm sitting at the bar of Chez Bella, the restaurant Natalie runs as head chef. I clasp the thick document in my hands, a mixture of excitement and terror churning in my stomach.

"It's official?" Natalie asks, sliding a piping-hot chocolate croissant in front of me.

"I signed the papers last night." It's nine in the morning, but I hand her one of the two glasses of champagne sitting in front of me. "Eight hundred square feet of wood and plaster are all mine."

We clink glasses. I gulp the champagne.

"You're America's lifestyle guru. Any co-op would be dying to have you." Natalie smiles and pushes a few stray blond hairs under her chef's hat. If only I could pull off hair that light, but I take after our father whose family is from the south of France near Italy: olive-ish skin (if I ever got out in the sun) and mousy-brown hair (if I ever kept it natural). God bless highlights.

"You should eat something." Natalie nudges the pastry toward me. Ever since I came out of the womb, Natalie has been trying to feed me.

"I'm too anxious." I move the offending pastry away. Food would not mix with the circus inside my stomach. "It's just dawned on me that I have a mortgage. And property taxes. And maintenance fees."

"Don't worry. You have a great job with the magazine and the new gig on *Wake Up, America!* Not to mention the money that's still coming in from your book."

"*Our* book."

Natalie waves her hand as if this is an insignificant fact. How can she be so flippant? If my life falls apart, hers will crumble too. We're balancing on a house of cards, and Natalie is the ace up my sleeve keeping it together.

"Did the board ask anything about your husband?" Natalie puts air quotes around the last word.

"Since the mortgage is in my name only, they didn't ask too many questions. I explained that he mainly worked out of the country, and I'd be the main resident. And once I got them on the topic of *Wake Up, America!*, all they wanted to talk about was what Holly Jenkins was like in real life and if

Ed Priestly really wore a toupee. My work at the magazine hardly came up."

"What's another lie on top of so many?"

"I know. I'm worried how naturally it comes now."

One of Natalie's underlings beckons from the kitchen, and she disappears. Her drink sits untouched, and I finish it in one swallow.

The thing is, my whole life is built on a lie. No, a lot of lies.

Lie Number One: I can cook.

It all started out so small. When I first began my lifestyle and interior design blog, *Blooming in the City*, I wanted to post some recipes along with my design tips. I asked my sister, Natalie, who was in culinary school at the time, for some original dishes, and she happily provided them. At the time, no one read my blog except my mom and her friends, so what did it matter. Right?

Then *The Huffington Post* picked up one of my posts—"10 Design Hacks I Wish I'd Done When I Was Twenty-One"— and suddenly my blog blew up. My new exposure led me to a chance meeting with Patrick Simon, now my editor at *Simply Chic*, and two weeks later, I was hired at the magazine.

As my popularity grew, I soon discovered you can't be the "Martha Stewart of the next generation" without including tips on cooking and meals and party planning, so I began adding more and more recipes and menus in the features I wrote for the magazine. I told Natalie what I needed, and she gave me the recipes. Through no fault of my own, my readers just assumed I could make all those gourmet dishes. I was only passing on information! It's not my fault they think I can actually cook them.

Lie Number Two: I'm a Domestic Goddess.

Give me a blank room and I can throw beautiful paint on the walls, fill it with chic furniture that dazzles the eye, and transform it into a masterpiece of modern design. Ask me to maintain it, clean it, and keep it organized—as I expertly advise my readers every month—and I fail every time.

If my readers opened my closets, looked under my bed, or peeked in one of my drawers, they would see I'm a fraud. Yes, on the surface, I can put together a beautiful home. I just can't keep it that way. I stuff drawers with papers I should file, old electronics cords, dead batteries, dried-up pens, and knick-knacks I'll never use. Ski clothes, old tennis shoes, books I've never read, and magazines I plan to reread are shoved under my bed. The closets have piles of clothes that need ironing, designer shoes that I plan to sell on eBay (if I ever get around to it), handbags shoved on top of winter coats, shoved on top of filing boxes, shoved on top of designer sheets that don't fit my new king-size bed.

If I didn't (discreetly) hire a cleaning lady, there would be inches of dust and dirt all over the counters, windowsills, and wood floors.

But every month, I write tips on how to keep a clean, efficiently run, organized home. Despite pets, kids, and husbands. None of which I have. And still, I leave my unpacked suitcase in a corner for months after I've returned from a trip.

Any time guests come to my home, I have to lock all the closets and cabinets. The only part of my home that is a wonder of organization is the kitchen pantry. It is systemized, labeled, and color coordinated. I spent an entire weekend using every hack I ever wrote and organized it to perfection. Since I never cook, it never gets used. It's like a museum piece. And I always "accidently" leave it open for any gawking guests.

Lie Number Three: I have a husband.

Okay, this one is easy to explain. I flat-out lied. Readers kept e-mailing and asking for advice on how to keep a house clean and organized in spite of a messy husband, or how to get their husband to help out with the cooking/laundry/cleaning, or what gift to buy a husband. So I started a section called "Husband Emergency." And suddenly everyone assumed I was married, and I went with it. I never mention my husband in particular, but I guess talking about husbands *in general* makes people think you have one. I figured that's their problem, not mine. It wasn't a big deal until I was hired as a legitimate writer for a legitimate magazine at a legitimate publishing house.

I never expected to get a book deal three years after being hired, *Catelyn Bloom's Guide to Living Simply Chic*— number eighteen on *USA Today*'s Best-Selling Books list— and I certainly never expected to be a guest correspondent on *Wake Up, America!*

It all just got out of hand.

The truth is probably pretty easy to figure out—this is the Internet age—but nobody has thought to doubt me. And my social media presence has almost always been exclusively about my blog and now the magazine. I've never been one to plaster my weekend plans all over social media. I'd rather plaster a room with designer wallpaper and share that on Facebook or Pinterest.

My phone pings, and I scrape through my tote until my hand clasps it, knowing there's only one person who would text me this early in the day. And I'm right. It's a text from my editor, Patrick.

Where are you??

I text back my location.

Be there in five. Don't move.

Only two people at work know the truth, and Patrick is one of them. I kinda slipped it in right after he got engaged to his now wife, Avery. The news that half of what I wrote was basically a lie hardly fazed him. He was too focused on his upcoming nuptials and the honeymoon.

As a thank-you, or as he calls it, entrapment, I asked him to edit my book when I signed my book deal. The publishing company wasn't too pleased, but they hired him as a freelance editor when I made it clear it was a deal breaker. I didn't want to involve anyone else in the lies. Now he's part of the conspiracy (his words, not mine) and not just an innocent bystander. But the fee he received covered the cost of his honeymoon, so I think we're even.

Patrick tumbles through the door, his tall figure slumped inside his gray overcoat. I slide the untouched croissant to him as he sits on the metal stool next to me. Under the two blotches of red on his cheeks from the cold, his face is pale, and I'm worried something has happened with Avery. For the past two months, his wife's been pumped full of fertility drugs, and about a week ago she went in to have the embryos transferred.

"Is Avery okay?"

"Huh? Oh, yeah. She's great." Patrick shoves half the pastry in his mouth. "You know that Good Samaritan who's been making headlines?" Flakes fly out of his mouth as he rushes on. "The travel writer who was almost killed when he saw a girl being kidnapped in Greece and followed the kidnappers and rescued her?" My blank stare prompts him to continue. "And when he woke up in the hospital, he didn't remember anything about his life. He has no parents—they died when he was a kid—and he's been working overseas for the past six months. Ringing any bells?"

"That's so sad." I really need to watch the news. Or check Twitter. "What happened?"

"I can't believe you work in media."

"I write for a lifestyle magazine."

Patrick shakes his head, looking like a disappointed father.

"Why are you telling me all this?" I ask.

Natalie sweeps by, accepting a delivery of fruits and vegetables. "Hi, Patrick."

"This croissant is spectacular, as always."

THE MISADVENTURES OF CATIE BLOOM

"It'll be featured in Catie's next food blog."

"I didn't hear that!" Patrick yells after her as she carries the boxes into the kitchen. He scrapes his hand through his short dark hair, making it stick up like a porcupine. "We're so screwed."

Patrick is always so dramatic.

"I'm on pins and needles here," I say.

"The guy, Max Euston, is Gillian Kennedy's nephew." Patrick lets this sink in. "She's been talking to the producers of *Wake Up, America!*, and they want to bring a film crew into your home to shoot a special segment as part of their *Coming Home* series in two weeks."

"Why my home? Can't they shoot the segment in the studio?"

"Gillian wants Max to have a larger-than-life homecoming in the home of the 'Queen of Domestic Bliss.'"

"Okay, but I'll need some help getting my new apartment together in time. It should be good publicity."

"You don't get it. She wants this poor guy to have a proper homecoming surrounded by family and home-cooked meals for an entire weekend. *Your* family. As in you, your husband, your gourmet cooking, and all the Catelyn Bloom fixings."

"But I don't cook."

Patrick looks at me and waits.

"And I don't have a husband!"

"I knew this would come back to bite us in the ass one day." Patrick rubs his eyes with the palms of his hands.

"I'll just tell Gillian no. I'll make up some excuse." My mind is already whirling. "I barely moved in, there are still boxes all over the place. I'll say a pipe burst and flooded the whole place. Or the floors are rotting. It'll be fine."

"Gillian doesn't understand no."

"Oh, please. I can charm anyone to say yes to anything." I bat my eyes at Patrick. "It works with you."

"Because I'm a wuss."

"When's the meeting?" I ask, undaunted.

"Two."

"Don't worry." I smile, patting Patrick on the back. "I've got this."

Chapter 2

CATIE

"What's her extension?"

Hovering over the phone at my desk, I'm suddenly not sure I can pull this off. To be honest, the few times Gillian Kennedy has powered through our offices, I ran to the break room and hid. She doesn't just own *Simply Chic*, she owns the entire media empire, Kennedy Media Corp. She's rich and powerful and a tiger.

"I can't do this." My face falls onto the mound of papers on my desk.

"Do what?"

I look up. Sam Harding's tall figure leans against my doorframe, his button-down shirt suspiciously familiar.

"Weren't you wearing that yesterday?"

A knowing smile crosses his face.

"What happened to all those clean shirts you keep in your office for occasions such as these?" I frown.

"I used the last one on Friday and forgot to replenish."

Patrick and Sam high-five over my head. It's so annoying how perfectly Sam fits into his role as the managing editor at *Edge Magazine*, "for the adventure-sports enthusiast."

"I don't have the energy to berate you this morning."

"What happened? You look upset."

If I didn't know better, I'd think there was genuine concern in Sam's voice. But I know better.

"Have you heard of the Good Samaritan the media's been salivating over? Max something?"

Sam nods.

"Well, he's Gillian's nephew, and she wants me to host him at my home for some big homecoming special for *Wake Up, America!* with my husband. And my fabulous cooking skills."

Sam's the second and final person at the office who knows my secret. He got me drunk one night and pried the truth out of me. Actually, he just asked, and I was so wasted I didn't even hesitate.

My assistant, Kyle, is heading toward me with a large box. He wobbles, avoiding the maze of files and interior design magazines piled around the floor of my office. I stand and help him set it down next to the dozen identical boxes against the wall of my small office.

"What are those?" Sam moves a stack of cookbooks off the Grant Featherston armchair in front of my desk and sits.

"Litter boxes."

Sam's dark eyebrows knit together in a question mark.

"In my last blog, I mentioned that the only reason I don't own a cat is because I'd have to clean up after it. Now all the cat-lovers are sending me self-cleaning litter boxes."

"Catie." Patrick points his eyes to my phone.

"I know. I know."

Deep breath. Deep breath. I can do this. Just dial the number.

"Catelyn Bloom for Ms. Kennedy." There are two clicks, and then Gillian is on the phone.

"Ms. Bloom, this saves me a call. The meeting has been moved up. Charles and his team from *Wake Up* are in the elevator as we speak. Be in my office in five minutes."

12

She hangs up, and I slowly sit back, chewing the crimson lipstick off my bottom lip.

"What happened?" Patrick is looking at me expectantly.

Sam has an annoying grin on his face.

"I couldn't get a word in." I stick my cell phone in the front pocket of my red pencil skirt. "She wants to meet now."

Patrick hurries after me. "You have to get out of it. I can't be fired. Think of Avery and all our fertility bills. And the new baby! If it works. It isn't cheap trying to get knocked up these days!"

Damn. Why'd he have to mention that? Doesn't he know I feel guilty enough as it is?

"Don't worry. I'm much better in person." I give him a thumbs-up and hurry to the elevator.

***

Straightening my shoulders, I march into Gillian's office, her wiry, red-haired assistant leading the way. A small conference table sits in an alcove at the far end of the expansive space. Gillian is seated on the other side of the mahogany table in a bright-green pantsuit with a comically large scorpion brooch on her lapel. To her left sits a crisply suited man in his fifties and Karen, the executive producer of *Wake Up, America!*

After a quick introduction, I place my hands on the back of one of the leather conference chairs, standing. "Good morning, everyone," I begin. "Thank you for this amazing opportunity. But—"

"I knew you'd be pleased. Poor Maxie. He hasn't had a real home since he was thirteen. And when Charles"—the suited man with a stiff tie and stiffer smile lifts his face to me—"suggested he be featured in their *Coming Home* series, I knew you were the perfect girl for the job. What's more heartwarming than a homecoming with America's favorite wife and homemaker?"

It takes me a moment to realize she means me.

Sure, in my made-up world I'm a perfect wife and happy homemaker, but in real life, I like to think of myself as a hip, youngish career woman living a fabulous life in the big city. I forget sometimes that my public sees me differently. And my boss.

"I'm so honored, but I can't host him. You see, um…" Four clenched faces stare at me, and I resist the urge to chew my lip. "I just signed the papers for a new apartment and I, er, we won't have time to unpack all the boxes, let alone have it ready for filming in two weeks."

Starting with the truth seems like a good idea—a bit foreign, but good.

"We won't be filming in your apartment," Charles Friedman states, the midday sun creating dark shadows around his face as it pours in from the wall of windows behind him. "The show's renting a townhouse in Brooklyn to use as your home."

"Wait. What?" My hands dig into the smooth leather of the chair I still stand behind. "Ms. Kennedy, you can't allow this. What about…"—what is it she always harps on about in her company memos?—"honoring the readers with the veracity of our work and image?"

"In my employees, I expect nothing but integrity. This is different."

"But the special is being promoted as a homecoming special at my home, and it won't be my home. Isn't that the same as lying? We can't have one of your beloved writers lying to her public."

Oh, God, don't strike me down.

"Sit, Ms. Bloom." Gillian's lips pinch together in a frown. I sink into the soft leather seat, feeling swallowed up.

"You won't be lying," Charles explains, placating me. "It will be promoted as a homecoming special *with* Catelyn Bloom and her family. There's nothing that states it will be at your house. We do this kind of thing all the time. It's a minor detail." The matter apparently settled, he continues, "We'll send you the location and the itinerary in a few days. Karen will be your contact person." Karen looks up, her green eyes hover over my face but in a flash are back on the iPad she's been tapping notes into during the meeting. Charles pulls out a folder, flipping it open. "The shoot will be pretty straightforward; we'll capture moments with you preparing meals and giving details about the recipes and other cooking tips as you entertain Max. There will be the homecoming dinner, an in-depth interview, a welcome-home party, and of course lots of moments of Max with his beloved dog surrounded by your family. Sound good?"

Not waiting for my answer, Charles rolls his chair out. Karen follows, shoving her feet into her black Havaianas flip-flops, even though it's forty degrees outside.

"Wait!" I yell, heat shooting up my neck. "But I…we can't do it if there's a dog there. My husband's allergic."

"Your husband can take a Benadryl." Gillian dismisses my concern.

"Uh, he can't. He's also allergic to antihistamines."

"The dog has to be there, Gilli." Charles exhales deeply, making it clear he's exhausted by my excuses. So am I, but a simple no isn't going to get me out of filming this special.

"It will be there." Gillian flicks her hand, dismissing the problem. "Your husband will be fine. We'll buy extra tissues."

"I don't think—"

"The dog is part of the deal. It's what convinced Max to do this special." Charles puffs air out of his mouth, exasperated. He continues slowly like I'm an idiot. It's humiliating being talked to like I'm a child, but I must sound like one as I frantically make excuse after excuse. "It's his childhood pet. Trixie was the first memory Max had when he started remembering things after the coma. Haven't you seen the photos plastered over every social media site?"

Fine, fine. He has some crazy attachment to his dog. Who cares? I still don't have a husband!

"Well, uh, my husband's a very private person. He won't like being filmed. In fact, he probably won't even be around. He has business out of state. Er, actually, out of the country."

There's a long silence in the room, and for a moment, I think I've taken care of one big problem. Now all I need is a quick 101 on cooking a large gourmet meal for a half-dozen people. I'm sure I can find some instructional videos on YouTube that will do. I can't ask Natalie to help—she'll be in Panama enjoying her first vacation in over a year.

"What's your husband's number?" Gillian has the phone in her hand, ready to dial.

"Wait! I, uh— I should talk to him first."

"I know what's going on here." Charles shoots his eyes at me, and my breath hitches in my throat. "You want more money."

My cheeks burn crimson. "No. No. I—"

"Then what's the problem?" Gillian places her hands on the slick table in front of her, giving me a look that makes me shrink down into my seat. "You're not the only lifestyle blogger out there. I was just on the phone with Candy Morgan's agent. They're looking to expand her profile, and she'd jump at this opportunity."

The name sends a shiver down my spine. Candy Morgan won one of those overly produced home-decorating-contest shows and has been popping up all over the lifestyle scene. I can feel her nipping at my heels.

"No!" I clear my throat. "It's fine. I'll talk to my husband. I'll work it out."

"We can't have any delays." Charles skips his eyes over Gillian and glares down at me. "Is this settled?"

Before I can answer, Gillian butts ins. "Of course it is, Charlie. Everything will run smoothly. I'll be there during the shoot to make sure of it." She stands, and as if she's the Queen of England, we all do the same, except Charles. "Thank you, Ms. Bloom."

Before I can utter another word, her secretary is guiding me out of the office.

This is bad. This is very bad.

Okay. There's always a solution. But it's not like I can just post an ad for a rent-a-husband. Or could I?

No. No. No way.

With my luck, I'll end up with some lunatic who would kill me in the middle of the night.

The shrill ring of my phone makes me jump. It's Patrick. I hit decline.

How am I going to break the news to him that not only did I fail but I need to find a husband and learn to cook in two weeks, or we'll both be fired?

Chapter 3

NATALIE

"What floor is your apartment on?" I yell into the phone that's gripped between my shoulder and ear, my hands occupied by two brown paper takeout bags heavy with food.

"Eighth. No, ninth. No, er…eighth. Eighth!" Catie sounds like she has marbles in her mouth, which means she's been drinking. A lot. The wood-paneled elevator glides smoothly to the eighth floor, and I walk down the softly lit hallway to Catie's new apartment. There are fresh lilies on a table at the end of the long corridor. It's a vast improvement from Catie's former fourth-floor walk-up, which reeked of rotting trash from the bins in the entryway where creatures of differing sizes and forms greeted you. I used to hold my breath, shield my eyes, and run for the staircase.

Inside the bright apartment, Catie and Patrick sit against the far wall in the open-plan living room, moving boxes surrounding the pair, a whiskey bottle between them. Half the boxes have been torn open, the contents scattered on the floor, as if Catie dug out the one item she needed and left the mess created by her search.

When she sees me, Catie offers me the whiskey bottle, but I decline. Her usually perfectly put together appearance is in disarray. Her usual silky hair is in a greasy bun, pieces sprouting out in all directions. The usual shimmer in her large, dark-chocolate eyes has turned lackluster. From the state she's in, tomorrow I'll be nursing Catie back to sobriety with fresh ginger and carrot juice and my specialty, banana-pecan waffles with bacon-infused maple syrup. This is my last week working at Chez Bella, and then I'm off to my mom's serene beach villa in Panama to decompress. When I return to the city, my life will be completely saturated by the renovations and business plans for the new restaurant I'm opening in Greenpoint, Brooklyn. I have one investor and hopefully another signing on soon, but the business is in a holding pattern right now as we wait on the permits for the renovations to come through.

But watching Catie now, I have a sinking feeling my life will be taken over next week, dealing with her latest calamity. There must be some way to get Catie out of this mess with her job intact. If it ever came out that I was helping my sister fraud the American public, I'm not sure how it would affect my future restaurant endeavors, and I don't want to find out.

"How long have you two been drowning in that bottle?" I slide the food bags onto the bar countertop that separates the kitchen from the living area. Catie's head is resting against the wall, her eyes closed, as Patrick stares down the long neck of the whiskey bottle.

"Not long enough."

Whiskey spills over the top of Catie's glass, and she shrugs, as if to say *I'll deal with it later*. She won't. I grab a napkin from the takeout bag and wipe the floor clean. Otherwise, it will be there until she moves again. Catie's living spaces always look gorgeous at first glance, but under the surface, they're pigsties. If you know where to look.

"You need food."

When Catie's texts started looking like hieroglyphics, I whipped up some truffle pasta, steak frites, and crème brûlée and left Jacques, the sous chef, in charge at Chez Bella. In a week's time, he'll be taking over as head chef, and he's already assumed most of the responsibilities. All that was left to do when I left earlier was finish the prep for tomorrow's brunch. Weekend brunch is busier than weekend dinner these days, thanks to Catie mentioning Chez Bella in a recent feature about brunch in cities around the nation. It was an unspoken thank-you, since I provided the recipes for *Catelyn Bloom's Guide to Living Simply Chic* and received no credit.

But Catie was true to her word, and I receive half the profits from the book sales, and that's how I'm able to finally open my own restaurant, which I've dreamed about since I was a kid. Catie's career is the best thing that ever happened to me.

A phone pings on the counter. It's Catie's, but she either doesn't hear it or doesn't care. Glancing at the screen, I see a message from Sam—*voulez-vous coucher avec moi ce soir?*—and smile at his persistence. He's been trying to get my sister to go out with him ever since he met Catie four years ago.

"Sam texted."

"What does he want?"

"To sleep with you."

Catie stands, snatches the phone, reads it, and hands it back, dropping her head on the bar. "He's sent me that same text every week since I met him."

"Every week for four years?" I press.

"Well, there was that nine-month period he kind of had a girlfriend. He stopped sending them until they broke up. Then he was back at it the day he kicked her to the curb." Catie points an off-kilter finger at me to make her point. "He does it to annoy me."

Catie always feigns disgust for Sam, but I know her feelings go deeper for him than she lets on. I have no idea if she would ever want him in her life as more than a friend—we both know what a heartless player he can be with the opposite sex, but she trusts him. I realized this the moment she told me she'd divulged her secret to him. She says she was wasted and her defenses were down. But it doesn't matter how drunk she was—when she has a secret, she clamps down on it like an iron vise. She would only reveal it if she completely trusted the person, and Catie rarely trusts anyone from the male sex. Not since college.

Picking up the phone, I type a response.

"Hey! What did you do?" Catie reads what I wrote, which is the location of Catie's apartment. "Nat, he's just looking for a booty call. He has, like, a list of women he goes through every night until one sorry girl accepts. Right, Patrick?"

"'S right." He's staring at his own phone as if it might bite him. Ever since Catie revealed that she wasn't able to get out of the special, he's been working up the courage to tell his wife the bad news.

I pull a bottle of Chardonnay from one of the bags and unscrew the top. Glancing around, I find a box on the kitchen counter labeled Glasses. Tearing the tape off, I pause. Half the glasses are broken. It looks like they were haphazardly stacked in the box with no padding or bubble wrap to protect them. I smile inwardly, remembering Catie's article last month titled, *Damage Control: The Art of Packing.* Gingerly, I take out two coffee mugs that are unscathed. I fill one with wine and one with water and place the water in front of Catie.

"Drink."

Catie rolls her eyes—a look I've witnessed ever since Catie was a little girl—but drinks the water in one go. I fill it again.

Patrick's phone starts vibrating, and he quickly slides up the wall. "It's my wife." Phone to his ear, he trudges down the short hallway and into the bedroom, shutting the door.

I grab hold of Catie's shoulders, making her dark hair fall around her face in a curtain. "You have to do something, Little Bee."

"Like what? I'm in too deep." Catie shrugs my hands off.

"What about an escort service or something?"

"Too risky. Not with the filming," she says, looking past me at the white-brick fireplace across the room. "Do you think a gilt mirror would look good above the mantel? Or maybe Tiffany Blue to give an unexpected pop of color?"

I snap my fingers in front of her face. "Catie. Focus."

A cold wind rushes across my shoulders from the open window, and the door buzzer jars me. Not bothering to ask who it is, I press the buzzer. A few minutes later, Sam walks through the door pulling the cap off his flop of dark hair, He wears slim tracksuit pants and a black dri-fit top that's snug against his impressively carved-out muscles.

"You're looking lovely tonight, Nat."

Sam kisses my cheek, which deepens in color. Despite Catie's constant warnings that Sam likes his women how he likes his assistants—easy, resourceful, and out of his sight when she's served her purpose—I like him. I know he's a heartbreaking playboy, but he's always been sweet and generous to me. He is trying to get into my sister's pants, but still.

"Catie, you look delicious, as always." His lips move to her cheek, but she snaps her face away, and he ends up kissing her ear. "I'm guessing it didn't go well with Gillian." Sam slides the six-pack of Stella he brought into the fridge, taking one out and popping the cap off in one quick motion.

"Horribly. The execs from *Wake Up* had a solution for every problem I threw at them, and Gillian wouldn't take no for an answer." Catie gulps from my wine. "Patrick's breaking the news to his wife now." She looks around at the boxes and pops her lip out in a pout. "All I wanted to do over the next two weeks was decorate my new apartment."

"There must be some way out of this mess. Let me help." Sam moves three boxes labeled Clothes together, and we each sit on one. I sink into the middle of my box.

"There's nothing to do. As soon as Gillian finds out I've been lying this whole time, she'll fire Patrick and me." Catie grasps the side of her box, steadying herself.

"You need to eat." I wiggle to standing and snap the lid off the pasta container. Then I tear apart a piece of brioche and place the pasta and bread in Catie's hand along with a fork. "Eat."

Even as a child, Catie could never eat during stressful times. I was the opposite. Food soothed me. Not the eating it as much as the creating something beautiful and delicious out of nothing. I inherited it from my mother and my dad's mom, my *mamé*. Their love of cooking was the only thing my mother and grandmother agreed on. They had a typical highly charged mother-in-law–daughter-in-law relationship. Until my father passed away. Then the two were inseparable, consoling each other in their mutual grief.

Catie scoops a small bite of pasta into her mouth and then puts the container on the ground next to her. "My stomach is in knots."

Sam picks it up, twirling pasta onto the fork and stuffing it into his mouth. "Damn, this is good."

I smile. Nothing makes me feel higher than being complimented on my food. "It's on page fifty-two of Catie's book. It's one of the most popular recipes, according to Amazon reviewers."

"You're a saint for giving Catie all those recipes for the book."

I shrug. "The recipes were only a small part of the book. The rest was all Catie. She has a gift for interior design."

Sometimes I wonder what the hell I'm doing still helping Catie, but every time I think about my new restaurant, I know it's all worth it.

"We've worked so hard to get here and now…it's over," Catie mumbles into her black mohair sweater.

Sam takes her hand, moving his thumb back and forth across her knuckles. "I'll take care of you."

"I'm not in the mood for jokes."

"At least let me take you away for a while. A few days alone with me and you'll forget everything." Sam smiles a wicked grin. How Catie can keep rejecting this gorgeous man, I can't fathom. If he looked at me that way once, I'd melt into his arms. Even if it was only for a night.

As I take a sip of my wine, a thick manila envelope on the counter catches my eye. I read the name on the return address and gasp.

"Catie, you could ask…," I flick my eyes to the envelope, but Catie vehemently shakes her head.

"Not an option."

"But—"

"No." Catie practically yells it.

It was silly to think Catie would go for it. It has been years since she's opened that can of worms, even if it would have been the simplest way out of this situation. Simple, but a lot of baggage and history to go along with it, plus I have no idea if Catie has even healed from that time in her life. Glancing for other clues on the envelope, I wonder what is inside, but it's blank except for the addresses.

Dropping the matter, I glance at Sam, who is arching his neck to read the envelope. An idea that has been circling in the back of my mind since he texted pops to the front of my thoughts. Sam will do anything for Catie, no matter what his motives are.

"Oh my God. That's it!" I stand, clapping my hands. "You *should* take her away! Across the bridge to Brooklyn.

Just the two of you, a Good Samaritan, and a TV crew. I'll…I'll put together a menu for the special and train Catie how to make each dish. Nothing too complicated. *Wake Up* should provide you with an assistant to help with the prep work. You've done it a million times before on the video blogs and *Wake Up, America!*" I kick the box Sam sits on, causing him to fall to his knees.

Sam looks at me bewildered, and then a knowing smile creeps on his face, and he sets down the food container, taking Catie's hand. "My darling, Catie, will you marry me?"

"Oh, no. No, no, no, no. We'll never pull this off." Catie wiggles out of Sam's grasp.

"It's only for two days." A rush of adrenaline speeds through my veins. My instincts were right. Sam loves a good game. Especially one that involves my sister. "It'll be an adventure."

"It'll never work. I've never cooked without you helping me, Nat. And what happens when the special airs, Sam? Your friends and family will know I'm a fraud. Someone will say something."

"I'll make them only film me from the back or something." Sam is bouncing in his sneakers, a wide grin on his face.

"They'll never accept that."

"They don't care about me. All they want to see is the perfect Catelyn Bloom hosting that poor sap. Did you ever see Martha Stewart's husband on TV when they were together? No. Your husband is meant to be background noise in your perfect life. Besides, it's only a ten-minute segment."

"Martha Stewart's been divorced since the eighties. Long before the Internet age. And ten minutes on morning TV is like an hour on prime time. Four million people watch the show. It's too risky."

The bedroom door bangs open, and Patrick walks in, his face collapsed.

"What did your wife say?" Catie asks, pulling away from Sam.

"I couldn't tell her. She started talking about baby names."

Three confused faces stare at Patrick.

"Avery's pregnant."

"Congratulations!" Catie hugs Patrick, but his arms hang by his side, his face frozen. When Catie backs away and sees Patrick's expression, I watch her resolve quickly melt away. She can't say no now. Not with Patrick's future hanging in the balance.

I shoot Catie a look. It's do-or-die time.

"Okay. Okay." Catie throws her arms in the air, relenting. "I'll do it. But we'll never pull it off."

Chapter 4

CATIE

"I've got Myra Hoefer's assistant on the phone. She's asking if we still want the Marques chair for the *Wake Up* special." Kyle crosses the large loft, my cell phone in his hand, dodging the hundreds of red-and-white fuchsias carefully woven into long white vines dangling from the ceiling. The loft, which we use as a studio for major shoots, is filled wall to wall with items for the February cover we've been shooting all morning.

"Yes. And the console. The special is filming on November twenty-ninth and thirtieth, but we need it by the twenty-eighth. Tell her someone from *Wake Up* will be in touch with the details." Kyle lowers his chin and raises his eyebrows, giving me an I-already-know-all-this look. "Sorry. Sorry. No more micromanaging."

Unmuting my phone, Kyle presses it to his ear and scurries out of the room. I peer at the large iMac monitor on the table in the corner of the room as Jack Cavalli, the photographer, pulls up the last shots he took. "The far-right side of the dining table is getting blown out by the light from that window, and the vines are too dense."

Jack does the majority of the cover shoots, and I've worked with him dozens of times over the years. We've developed an easy, symbiotic relationship, and we work well together.

"I agree."

"Mike!"

Jack's assistant hovers behind us—an eager beaver always ready to leap into action—and shuffles a step closer. "Remove two dozen of the vines between the camera and the dining table."

As he carries a ladder from vine to vine, untying the delicate arrangements, I take a moment to look through the test shots, zooming in on the red and white cupcakes, the champagne glasses with raspberries floating on top, the red fabric draped over the backs of the white velvet dining chairs, the small black chalkboards at each seat with sugary-sweet phrases written on them, and the maroon jars of red and white carnations scattered over the table.

It's too busy.

I gather all the mason jars and place them in a pile at the edge of the studio, take a bite out of one of the cupcakes, and angle one of the dining chairs so it looks like someone has just left the table. The studio phone rings and I answer it, my mouth still thick with chocolate cake. "'Ello?"

"Catie, it's Karen."

"Yes." But the word sticks in my throat. Jack is one step ahead of me and hands me the bottle of water I was about to motion for.

"Hello? Hello!"

Taking three gulps, I clear the sweetness from my mouth. "I'm here, Karen."

"Good. I'm sending our set designer over to the townhouse tomorrow at noon. Can you be there?"

The hairs on the back of my neck prickle. "I told you I'm designing the rooms for the special. I don't need help from your designer."

There's a pause and muffled noises in the background. "That's fine. But Deidra, our set designer, will need to approve the designs." Before I can protest, Karen rushes on. "Shooting for TV is different than shooting for a magazine. She needs to make sure everything will work on camera. It's for your benefit."

"Fine. Fine. But if—"

"Great. We'll send a car to your office at ten thirty tomorrow to take you to Brooklyn." Karen hangs up.

Mike has cleared the excess vines, and Jack takes a couple of shots and studies them on the large iMac screen. He snatches a blackout curtain from the pile next to him, and Mike hangs it over one of the floor-to-ceiling windows. The studio is located on the top floor of our building, and the walls are constructed of exposed white brick with tall, arched windows on the north and east walls that let in loads of natural light. Jack hardly ever uses artificial lighting for his shoots. He moves the light around the room using blackout curtains and reflectors. Before I can comment on the new images, Kyle is back, the phone pressed to his ear.

"One moment." He covers the bottom of the phone and lowers his voice as he says to me, "It's Natalie."

I hesitate a moment and then take the phone, saying, "I'm running a little late."

"No shit, Sherlock. How late?" Natalie's breathing comes out in short puffs, and the sounds of traffic whooshing in the background muffles her voice.

"Where are you?"

"Two blocks away." A horn honks in the background.

"Set everything up in the test kitchen, and I'll be right down," I say. We shoot the video blogs in the test kitchen, so Natalie is familiar with it.

"How long?"

"Twenty minutes."

"Right. See you in forty-five." Natalie hangs up. I smile. She knows me too well. I hand Kyle the phone. "Did Patrick get back to me on the cooking tips I wrote up for the special?"

"Yes. He approved..." Kyle looks at the e-mail on his phone and reads, "'10 Cooking Hacks That Elevate Your Party From B-List to A-List,' '7 Easy Ways to Make a Homecoming Party Fabulous,' and 'The Perfect Special-Occasion Dinner Menu.'" Looking back at me, he adds, "And Karen called. She's mailing the contracts for you and your husband and needs them signed and back to her by the end of the week."

"Why?" My heart picks up speed. Kyle doesn't know about my lies. He's never questioned why my husband is suspiciously absent. To keep any doubts at bay, I send red roses to myself every Valentine's Day, I cringe every time they arrive, and I never say they are from my husband, but I figure Kyle assumes that's who sends them every year. If he suspects anything, he's never said. Honestly, I don't think he cares about my personal life. He's paid well, treated with respect, I almost never keep him late or on weekends, and I often slip him freebie products we receive. It's a cushy job. I make sure of it. The last thing I need is a new assistant sniffing around, asking a lot of questions.

"I don't know," he says. "I can call and ask her."

"No. No." I usher him to the door. "I'll take care of it. Go make sure Natalie gets through security and has everything we need in the kitchen."

After Kyle leaves, Jack snaps several test shots around the dining table, and we look over them until we agree on the best angle. I make a few adjustments to the decor, he snaps several shots, and after reviewing them again, we're done with the shoot.

"Wait." I walk over to the table and begin hacking the cupcakes apart. They crumble into a pile and fall in sad clumps beside the tiered tray they rested on. "We need to take a few more shots for the digital edition. Jaclyn, the digital editor, wants to do an anti-Valentine's day piece. It'll only take a few minutes."

I instruct Mike to hack away at the vines, leaving half hanging in shreds and half in piles spread across the wood floor. I add *bitter* in front of the word *sweet* on one of the mini chalkboards and cross out *you* and add *me* to make another board read "I love me." I break two plates on the floor and yank at the tablecloth so everything on the dining table is askew.

Jack takes a couple test shots, and we look at the screen, then try a few more angles, move the vines on the ground around, and snap a couple more pictures. Once we get everything just right, I tell him to get his camera ready, and then I tip two champagne glasses over and the liquid spills to the floor. Jack quickly *click, click, clicks.* The cascading liquid is captured perfectly, glistening in the midday sun as it drips to the floor. Then he snaps a few shots of specific items on the table: the tray of smashed cupcakes, the broken plates, the torn vines, and the knocked-over chair.

"I'll review them and send the shots to you and Jaclyn by the end of the day," Jack says.

I grab my bag and race toward the door, skidding to a stop as Sam saunters in, Ray Bans and a bright-white smile on his face. "I thought this was a Valentine's Day shoot, not the Valentine's Day Massacre," Sam says, looking behind me at the beautiful disaster.

"Valentine's Day is always a bloody massacre," I shoot back.

"I should have words with your husband. He's obviously failing at his job." Sam slides his arm around my waist and squeezes my ribs, making me squeal in spite of myself.

"Knock it off," I say, shooting my eyes in Jack and Mike's direction. "I'm late meeting Natalie in the kitchen." Sam releases me and follows me out of the studio and into the elevator. His hand slides into mine. "Stop it."

"If you can't even handle my hand in yours, how are we going to pass as man and wife?"

"It'll be different when the cameras are rolling. I'm quite a good little actress."

"I'm aware. But it won't just be for the cameras. We'll basically be living as man and wife during the weekend we're shooting the special. It's not just for the cameras. It's for the crew and executives and Gillian. Everyone will be watching us."

His hand finds mine again, and I slap it away. Anger and hurt curtain his face as the bell dings and the elevator doors slide open. Patrick stands on the other side.

"Oh, God, this is never going to work," he says, his shoulders tensing as he takes us in. "You two look like you're about to kill each other."

I hurry down the hall, Sam and Patrick behind me. "Good. We'll be just like most married couples I know."

"You're too young to be this bitter," Patrick says. "What happened? Father issues?"

"My dad died before he could do any damage."

Patrick's ruddy cheeks pale at my words.

"Don't worry. It was a long time ago. My bitterness has nothing to do with daddy issues."

"First love?" Patrick tries again.

My heart freezes in my chest, but I force my feet to keep moving.

"She's a hot mess." Sam nudges Patrick's shoulder as I reach the door to the test kitchen.

"Don't act like you know anything about my love life."

"I know a lot more than you think." Sam raises his dark eyebrows.

THE MISADVENTURES OF CATIE BLOOM

Before I can quiz him, he pushes his way into the kitchen and gives a big hug to Natalie who is looking over a folder thick with recipes and notes. A grin extends across her face as she melts into his embrace. *Typical.*

"Have you narrowed down the menu?" Patrick asks Natalie.

As Natalie opens the folder and shows Patrick several recipes, I pull Sam aside.

"We have a problem. Karen is e-mailing the contracts for the special today. She needs you to sign them."

"Why me?"

"Because you're my husband."

Sam pauses, working his jaw. "Forward them to me when you get them."

"What about—"

"It's no big deal. It'll just be a standard contract." Sam walks back to the counter. "I'll sign it, and it will go in a file somewhere. No one will even look at them." His phone rings and he takes the call, stepping outside the room.

Okay, maybe it's not a big deal, but signing a legal document worries me. Not that we're doing anything illegal. At least, I don't think so. Deceiving the American pubic isn't illegal, but the media and the public would persecute us if the truth came out. Shaking my head, I try to forget the grave deception I'm embarking on and walk around the kitchen counter, running my hands over a black spatula, a wiry utensil, and something that looks like a squat metal hammer. *Let's just get this over with.*

"Catie, get your butt over here," Patrick yells, making me jump and drop the hammer thing to the floor with a loud *thunk.*

"I'm here. I'm here. Geez."

"Karen said they want shots of you preparing a welcome-home breakfast, making a party cocktail, and cooking the homecoming feast. *Wake Up* will share your menus and recipes on their website, and we'll do the same. I've already talked to Jaclyn about it." Patrick scans the recipes and menus Natalie has printed out. "Something simple like this overnight French toast and Gruyere scrambled eggs look great for the breakfast. It doesn't need to be fancy. It needs to be—"

"Simply chic," Natalie chirps, smiling.

"Exactly."

"Why overnight French toast?" I ask, looking over the recipes.

"It's Max Euston's favorite," Patrick says. "Gillian sent over a list of his favorite foods, and Natalie put the menu together based on that. For the homecoming meal, there needs to be at least five dishes for the main meal and one or two desserts." Patrick looks over a list of menu options. "This pumpkin-toffee cheesecake looks amazing. And you could do this simple apple pie. Wait, are you a baker or chef?"

"Chef," Natalie explains. "But our *mumé* loved baking and taught me several recipes growing up. I like baking. I just can't do the fancy decorating. My hands are too inept for precision work."

"The cake sounds complicated. Will I be able to do it?" I ask, squeezing in between Patrick and Natalie.

"We're about to find out." Natalie slides the recipe for the pumpkin cheesecake in front of me, which I glance at, as she pulls out ingredients from a grocery bag she's brought and hands a receipt to Patrick.

"Can't we just skip to the part where I dump all the ingredients together and put it in the oven?" My breathing quickens as I watch Natalie pull out over a dozen ingredients. "Is that all for the cake?"

"Cakes. You're making two of them." Natalie hands me the butter. "Remember, I'm not going to be there. I can do some prep before I leave for my trip, but you're going to mainly be on your own."

34

"What? No. *Wake Up* will have someone to assist me. I never have to prep the food when I go on the show. One of their lackeys always does it."

"With my help."

"What?"

"As far as *Wake Up* is concerned, I'm one of your assistants. They call me before each show, and I walk them through what you're making and what needs to be prepped and how. I've told you all this before."

I really need to listen more, but if it doesn't have to do with interior design, I have selective hearing. Relying on Natalie has become second nature.

"Well, you can still talk to them before you go and tell them everything that needs to be done."

Natalie's lips tighten. "But you still need to know how to make this cake—and all the recipes—from beginning to end, just in case something happens."

"Nothing's going to happen."

"Don't say that!" Patrick yells. "Don't ever say that. Are you trying to jinx us?"

The door swings open, and Sam walks back in, sliding his phone into his jeans pocket. I grab his arm and pull him next to me. "Pay attention in case I forget any of this."

"Now you touch me."

"Shut up," I say, his arm still warm in my hands. "It's both our butts on the line here."

There's a quiet knock on the door. Kyle peeks his head in. "WeHome is on the phone. What size do you want the blue-and-white rug? And the shag rug?"

Taking the phone, I quickly discuss the sizes and shapes of all the rugs I'll be using in the townhouse for the special, and then I hand it back to Kyle. "And Ms. Kennedy's assistant called and said they need to talk to you about the dog."

"What dog?" Sam asks. "No one said anything about a dog."

I widen my eyes to him in the universal shut-the-hell-up-or-you'll-give-us-away look. "Thanks, Kyle." I give him his exit, and off he scurries.

Sam looks like he wants to hurl.

"Don't tell me you're afraid of dogs." I laugh, but Sam's face is white. "There's going to be a greyhound there. Max's childhood pet."

"I don't think I can do it."

"You have to!" Patrick yelps. "I'll get you some hypnosis tapes or something."

"Greyhounds are the sweetest dogs, Sam." Natalie places a motherly hand on his shoulder.

Sam's phone beeps. "I have to go. I've got an interview with that new Aussie snowboarder in ten minutes. We'll talk about this later," Sam directs his comment at me.

"Is there snow in Australia?" Natalie asks.

"Not much. That's why it's a compelling story."

As Natalie begins measuring out the ingredients, Sam pulls me aside. He looks directly into my eyes. "I'm not thrilled about the dog, and I want to know more about it, but right now there's a bigger problem."

I press my lips together, waiting for another bomb to drop.

"We need to look natural together for the special. I'm not saying we have to be all lovey-dovey, kissing and holding hands all the time. But we need to be comfortable around each other, and you can't flinch if I put my hand on any part of your body."

"Any part?"

Sam's face hardens. "Jesus, Catie. I'm not a perv. I'm not going to grope you just because we're pretending to be married. Give me a bit of respect. I'm giving up a lot to help you out."

Chastened, I mumble, "Sorry."

"What? I didn't hear that?"

I laugh. "Sorry. I said I'm sorry. I know you're not going to be feeling me up every chance you get, but...you are *you*."

"And I'm pretty great." He swings the door open.

The door closes before I can yell out a snappy comeback. I butt heads with him, but Sam is turning his life upside down for me, and, yes, I know he loves any kind of adventure, but he is going out of his way to help me. My heart swells and presses against my ribs as I think of everything he's doing for me. Biting my lip, I mentally squeeze my heart back down. If I let it inflate too much, Sam will surely burst it in the end. I've seen him do it to every woman before me, and there have been many.

"Catie. Let's get a move on. I have to be at the restaurant in an hour."

Next to Natalie, I look over the ingredients, and she steps back, making me go through each step on my own. First, I mismeasure the salt. Anyone can mistake a tablespoon for a teaspoon. Nothing tragic. Then I put the mixer on too high, and batter sprays all over the counter, cupboards, and our clothes. Now there's orange goop all over my Miu Miu flats, dammit. Once the cakes are finally assembled, Natalie makes me start the toffee topping as they cook in the oven.

After the third time I burn the sugar for the topping, Natalie gives up. And when the buzzer rings to alert me the cakes are cooked, I reach in and pull one out, and Natalie stops me.

"Look at it. Do you think it's done?"

I jiggle it a bit. "I don't know. Isn't cheesecake supposed to be a little wiggly?"

"It's not a Jell-O mold." Natalie lets out a long sigh. "It's meant to be dense. It needs at least ten more minutes."

"Are you sure?"

"I've been doing this for ten years—I'm sure." She hands me a knife. "Stick it in the middle." I do as I'm instructed and when I slide the knife out, orange batter sticks to the end. "If it was done, the knife would come out smooth. It's baking 101."

"Okay. Okay. I'll make a note of it."

I put the cake back in the oven next to the other one and turn up the temperature.

"What are you doing?" Natalie practically yells.

"I have to get to a meeting in ten minutes."

"Turning up the temperature won't make them cook faster!" Her head drops onto the counter in exasperation. "It'll make them burn on the outside and undercook on the inside," she mumbles into the counter.

I turn the temperature down.

Picking her head up, Natalie exchanges a look with Patrick. "I'm cancelling my trip."

"What? No," I say. "I'll get this. It'll be fine. I just need more time."

"We don't have time. In one week, producers and cameramen will be surrounding you, and you've never done this on your own. Even when we film the video blogs, all you do is introduce everything and throw the prepared ingredients together. Any chopping, sautéing, or mixing is done in close-up by me. You'll ruin it. And then you'll ruin me." Natalie roughly arranges her notes back in the folder and snaps it shut.

I look at poor Patrick. Who am I kidding? He's going to have a baby. I can't risk it. I'd hate myself. If I'm getting through next weekend, I need Natalie by my side. "Thank you, thank you, thank you. I'll pay for any cancellation fees or anything that can't be refunded. I owe you one."

"You owe me a lot more than one, Little Bee."

My skin turns clammy as I suddenly realize I have everything I need to pull off this charade. So why don't I feel like jumping up and down to Katie Perry like I did when I got this job four years ago? Instead, my whole body has gone rigid. The thing is, I never really believed it would all come together for the special. I was moving forward at warp speed this past week, but I didn't consider what it would mean if I really did find a husband and got the cooking in order.

But now that it's all come together, and in record time, I have no idea if all the pieces will fit. It could all come crashing down as fast as it was built up, and my horrible fall will be captured by a national TV crew. But there's no turning back now. I have to go through with it. For the sake of everyone who's counting on me. And my new apartment. And my entire career.

But if it all implodes, I'll be the sorry fool on top of the sad mess, wondering what the hell happened to my perfect life.

Chapter 5

CATIE

"How did the walk-through go?" Natalie asks, sticking her head through the space between the front seats of the rental car as we drive over the Brooklyn Bridge on our way to the townhouse. It's Friday evening, and we're meeting the production crew at the house and setting it up for the early shoot tomorrow.

"It was tense. The schedule's tight, and the crew was annoyed to be working over the Thanksgiving holiday weekend to prepare for the shoot. Not that I blame them. But the house is gorgeous. A three-story brownstone, newly renovated, with a large backyard and patio, owned by a painter and her husband, a retired documentary filmmaker."

"How did *Wake Up* gain access to the house?" Natalie asks.

"Mr. Friedman knows the husband and asked if they could rent it for the shoot. The couple spends the winter in Costa Rica."

We hiccup down a cobbled road after we exit the Brooklyn Bridge and enter the quiet, tree-lined streets of Brooklyn Heights.

"When is the guest of honor arriving?" Sam asks as he flips through the stations. The car swerves, and I slap his hand off the radio.

"Eyes on the road." I settle back into the front passenger seat. "Gillian's meeting him at JFK now. They're coming straight here from the airport."

There's a picture of Max Euston attached to the itinerary I've pulled up on my phone. A young man with sharp features and serious eyes stares back at me. His hair is short, and he wears khakis and a camouflage jacket. He looks more like a soldier than a travel journalist.

The road has smoothed, and we turn right and then left onto Grace Court. Nearly identical brownstones line the quiet street on both sides, and the Hudson River sparkles at the end of the street where it dead-ends into a walking path. The sun is just falling behind the buildings on the far side of the river as we pull up outside the brownstone, which we'll use for the filming. Sam maneuvers the car back and forth into a spot in front of one of the buildings. My heart clenches, rising into my throat. I take several deep breaths until my heart rate slows. I've been living this charade for the past four years—what's another forty-eight hours, right?

"I thought it'd be nicer," Natalie says as she grabs a box of groceries from the trunk.

"Wait until we get inside. It's stunning." I stand, stretching my arms above my head.

Taking another box of groceries from the back seat, Sam leads us up the steep steps and opens the double doors. We follow him inside to the foyer. The ceiling soars above us, and directly in front of us stands a grand staircase with a glossy-black banister, and impressive white crown molding lines the edge of the high ceiling. A white-and-gold blown-glass pendant hangs above our heads. The entryway still takes my breath away, as it did last week when I met with the set designer here.

After opening a pair of tall white double doors to my right, we walk into the living room. The ceilings are twelve feet tall with the same crown molding lining the entire room. Two floor-to-ceiling windows bathe the room with light, and a gray stone fireplace dominates the south wall.

"That fireplace is bigger than my apartment." Natalie gawks.

Packed into the far corner of the living room are the accent tables, chairs, paintings, rugs, and other décor I've borrowed for the shoot. Thank goodness for the magazine. We have relationships with many of the top designers, who all jumped at the chance to have their pieces featured on *Wake Up, America!* Kyle spent the last week organizing the delivery of everything. Of course, the house came with its own beautiful designer furnishings and décor. When I walked through last week with the set designer, I indicated the pieces I liked in the living room, dining room, and kitchen—the rooms we're shooting in—and had the rest of the furnishings from those rooms stored in the attic.

Walking to a swinging door that leads to the kitchen, I hold it open for Natalie and wait for her reaction.

"Are you freakin' kidding me?!"

Laughing, I follow. I purposely neglected to tell her that the kitchen was a proper state-of-the-art chef's kitchen, with an eight-range gas stove and three ovens.

"I knew you'd love it."

Opening cabinets and drawers, Natalie is like a kid at FAO Schwarz, picking up and trying every new toy she finds. "I think I'm in love."

The doorbell draws Sam back out to the foyer. A few moments later, he rushes back into the kitchen, his eyes wide.

"What's the matter?"

"The dog's here."

"I thought he was coming down with Gillian and Max," I say.

Just then my phone rings. It's Patrick. I answer it.

"I forgot to tell you. Gillian had a problem with the dog," Patrick says in a rush.

"What do you mean?" I ask. Sam is nudging me out of the kitchen.

"It died."

"What?!" I halt.

"It had bone cancer, and it died suddenly last week. Gillian's assistant just called and said they found a rescue greyhound shelter that is sending over a dog right now."

"It's already here," I tell him.

"The assistant said Max can't know the dog is a foster dog. They scoured the region until they found a dog in Connecticut that looks just like the one he grew up with."

"Are you joking?"

I walk out the front door and see a skinny kid with a Mets hat standing in front of a navy van. He slides open the side door and out jumps a silvery-gray greyhound, which leaps forward and pummels me to the ground, my phone flying to the sidewalk.

I shove her back, but my arms become tangled with her hind legs and her front paws bat at my face. She's pulled off, and I roll to the side, only to be attacked again. The dog's tongue is on my cheek and ear, making me inadvertently laugh. I'm literally being smothered by love.

"Sit!" I yell.

She does sit. On me.

The kid in the Mets hat pulls her off me by the collar. As soon as I scramble to my feet, the dog bounds toward me again. I screech and race to the front door, the kid chasing the dog behind me. Sam is halfway up the staircase in the foyer, watching the events unfold through the open door. The kid drags the dog up the steps and into the foyer.

"Let's put her in the back for now." I lead the way through the kitchen and out onto the back patio. The kid releases the dog, and she bounds down the stairs into the manicured garden and patio.

"What happened?" Natalie is beside me with a bottle of sherry she's cooking with in her hand. I grab it and take a long gulp.

"I was just mauled by a dog."

Natalie fills a bowl with water and puts it outside.

The kid shoves a clipboard at me. "Just sign here and here. I'll be back for him Sunday afternoon." After dropping a bag of dog food in the pantry, the kid leaves.

"Why are you signing for Max's dog?" Natalie asks, wetting a tea towel and handing it to me.

"It's not his dog." I explain the strange phone call I received from Patrick a moment ago.

"That's not a dog—that's a lawsuit," Sam says, entering the kitchen, warily looking out the window.

"I can't believe you're afraid of dogs," I laugh.

"I hate dogs. But I love bitches." He kisses me on my sore cheek, making me wince. My face is raw from the dog's rough paws, and I gingerly pat it with the tea towel. God, I hope it's not too red. I can't be on TV with a messed-up mug.

Once my heart rate slows down, I leave Natalie to unpack the groceries and set up the kitchen, while I get to work decorating the living room and formal dining room, the two main rooms that will be used in the special. I've left the bedrooms untouched, since they will only be used as sleeping quarters.

Two hours later, the living room has been transformed. I've changed out the curtains, throws, rugs, and accent pillows and arranged the furniture so there is a cozy sitting area in front of the fireplace and a formal sitting area next to the tall windows along the front wall. In front of the fireplace there is now a McKenna white-linen sofa with silver nailhead trim. The Amici square coffee table is bookended by two silver-gray Louis XIV armchairs. The cool tones of the furniture pieces are a beautiful contrast with the warm cherry wood flooring in the long room. A blue-and-white wool-and-silk paisley rug brings it all together under the white coffee table.

The formal sitting area is framed by long dark-gray velvet curtains that pool at the floor. On the wall behind the sitting area is dark-pink damask acrylic wallpaper. The set designer from *Wake Up* had her crew put it up last week at my request. I love acrylic wallpaper. It goes on easily and can be changed out on a whim without damaging the wall. As a final touch, I've arranged fresh white and blue hydrangeas in glass vases throughout the room.

I take several pictures and send them off to Patrick.

He quickly replies. *Perfect. Let's hope you make the rest of the weekend look as effortless and beautiful.*

Ye of little faith, I respond.

Thanks to you, faith is all I got. Now go work your magic on the rest of the weekend.

Abracadabra, I reply.

That better not be my job disappearing!

I ignore his last text and slide the phone back into my pocket.

"You're an artiste." Sam walks into the room with two rolling suitcases behind him. "You really don't need the rest of it. You could focus on just interior design and still be just as successful." I ignore him. It's not the first time he's made a comment like this, but it's not like I can walk into Gillian's office and tell her I'm done with the cooking and organizing and only want to focus on design. It doesn't work that way. Not if I want to keep my job.

Pulling a piece of packing tape off the bottom of his shoe, Sam says, "Except for the mound of trash you've left in your wake." There are empty boxes, packing peanuts, and plastic wrap scattered throughout the room where I unpacked and unwrapped the furniture and décor.

I catch a glimpse of my face and hair in the round, gilt mirror above the fireplace. In less than an hour, Max will be arriving, and I need to freshen up my hair and makeup. "I'll deal with it later. I need to change before everyone arrives." Lugging my large suitcase up the front staircase, Sam follows with his small black roller bag.

"Who's sleeping where?" Sam asks as we reach the top of the stairs, a narrow hallway stretching in front of us.

Leading him down the white-and-navy-striped hallway, I indicate one bedroom after another. "Gillian will sleep here, Max in here, and Natalie will take the small room by the back stairs."

At the other end of the hallway is a large set of double doors that I open into the master suite. I kick off my shoes and sink my toes into a plush lambskin rug covering the dark wood floors. Dominating the room is a king-size canopy bed with downy-white bedding. In a large seating area that could be its own room are a loveseat and two armchairs facing two large windows overlooking the street.

"Isn't this amazing!" I gush.

"What's in there?" Sam indicates another set of double doors, pushing them open.

It's the master bathroom, complete with a Jacuzzi tub and a spa shower with his-and-her showerheads. The lighting is low, and the room has heated marble floors, dark wood paneling, and gray stone tiles lining the wall. A mix of mint, sage, and lavender fills my nose. It's small but better than any five-star spa I've ever experienced.

"This is all mine." I climb into the empty tub and stretch my legs out. Sam climbs in after me. The tub is cool, but his shoulder is warm against me.

"Ours, honey."

Wait. What?

"We're man and wife. We're expected to share the same room." Sam winks.

I bite my lip. When assigning bedrooms, I'd forgotten about Sam. I know what Freud would say, and he can shut it. There is no subconscious meaning to this little oversight.

"Or you can sneak out and share your sister's tiny twin bed once everyone is sleeping if you want," Sam deadpans.

I squeeze his thigh hard, and he yelps.

"Natalie and I can share the bed in here and you can take the twin bed." I smile. "It works out perfectly."

"Seriously, Catie. We're sleeping in the same room. I haven't risked my own career to have it all blow up in my face because of logistics." He jumps out of the tub. "If we're going to do this, we're doing it right. By my rules. Because it isn't a game. It's my life."

His dark eyes challenge me.

"Fine." I climb out of the tub and throw myself onto the master bed, sinking into the lushness. "But we're sleeping head to toe, and if I feel even a hair of yours near me, I'll knee you in the groin."

It's meant as a joke, but Sam crosses his arms over his broad chest, and I feel like a schoolgirl about to get a scolding.

"Is that really what you think of me? I like you, Catie. I've made that clear, but I'm not about to force myself on you. I've told you that. Do you believe me?" His demeanor is so severe; it's frightening and sexy all at the same time. "Answer me."

Damn.

"Yes. I believe you."

"Good. Because if you fuck this up, Gillian will fire me too."

"I know that."

The noise of a car stopping in front of the townhouse and a car door opening makes me start. Out the window, I

47

see a taxi idling at the curb and a young man in jeans and a dark-gray sweater climbs out. The doorbell chimes, and Sam and I walk downstairs.

My heart does a little skip as I open the door and see the handsome young man standing in front of me. It takes me a moment to realize it's Max Euston. He looks older than he did in his picture, and his clothes throw me. His brown hair has grown several inches, and his eyes have a wariness about them that the picture lacked.

"Hi. I'm Max Euston." He looks at a piece of paper in his hands. "I'm looking for Mrs. Catelyn Bloom."

"That's me. Catie." I step back, letting him enter.

"Oh." He looks disoriented.

"I'm Sam." His arm wraps possessively around my shoulders. "Catie's husband." Sam grabs my chin and presses his lips firmly against mine. "Sorry. Sometimes I feel like we're still newlyweds."

The kiss takes me by surprise, and when I recover, I give a forced laugh and elbow Sam in the ribs. "Don't mind him," I say to Max, who is staring at his feet. "My darling husband just gets carried away."

Before Sam can do any more damage, I put my hand on Max's elbow, leading him into the living room. "Let me show you around."

"Is Trixie here?" Max smiles brightly, the wariness I saw earlier gone. "I won't feel like I'm home until I see her."

Oh, God. I can't face the dog again.

"It should be about time for her walk. She loves going out at dusk," Max says.

We look out the window to the darkening sky.

"Well, I guess we better get a move on," I say.

I take Max through the kitchen and out onto the deck. I can't see the dog anywhere in the garden, and I realize I have no idea what the new dog's name is.

"Doggie," I whisper. "*Psst. Psst.* Doggie."

"Trixie!" The deep voice startles me. Max has come up beside me. "Bacon always does the trick when I can't find her. Do you have any?" Max looks expectantly at me.

"Of course."

He walks down onto the paved stones and around the small pathway that leads through the small landscaped garden.

"Let me just—"

"Why don't you two go inside and wait in the living room," Sam, who has been watching the scene quietly, says. "I'll get some bacon and look for her."

Eyeing Sam, I question his motives, especially since he's scared of the dog, but I let him play out his game, whatever it may be. In the kitchen, Sam asks Natalie for a piece of bacon, and I show Max into the living room.

"For some reason, I still don't feel like you fit in here. You look like you belong in a hip apartment in the city." Max sits on the plush white couch across from the fireplace, his back straight and his feet flat on the ground. "I guess I'm still picturing a Martha Stewart type, not a beautiful young woman."

Wow. He's really hot. And he just called me beautiful.

"Wasn't your aunt picking you up from JFK?"

"Sorry. I didn't mean to intrude. I—"

"No, no. I didn't mean that." I sit next to him. "I just wondered how you got here so early."

"Oh. I took an earlier flight and caught a taxi. I phoned Aunt Gilli, and she was already in a car on her way out to the airport. She turned around but said she needed to get a few things before she came to your house." Max looks out the window as the night begins to smother the daylight, even though it's only four in the afternoon.

"Well, uh, this isn't really my house. The studio is renting it. I guess they do that kind of stuff all the time. TV magic and all that."

"Yeah, reality and TV don't really mix," Max agrees. "That's why I got into journalism."

Wind rattles the window, and I give an involuntary shiver.

"Are you cold? I can start a fire. I saw some wood piled up next to the front steps, near the ground entrance." Max is already halfway to the front door.

"That would be great."

A few minutes later, Max comes back in, kicking off his boots, and dumps some logs into the fireplace, arranging them expertly and thrusting some crumpled newspaper and kindling from a nearby bin underneath the logs. He scrapes a match on the hearth, and the logs ignite into flames. Soon, a fire rages. Max pulls off his heavy sweater and jabs at the fire with a poker, his back muscles flexing under his tight T-shirt.

"I can't find the dog."

I'm startled by Sam's voice so close to me. His mouth is pulled into a frown. I doubt he even looked.

"Where could it have gone? The backyard has brick walls and fencing on all sides," I whisper, smiling at Max who has turned to look at us.

"I looked. But it's not there," Sam hisses back.

"Maybe it ran away."

"You better hope not."

"Keep looking," I say.

"You go look."

"I have to entertain our guest. I'm the whole reason he's here."

A shadow crosses over Sam's face, but it quickly disappears, and his hallmark smile returns as he says, "Don't forget you're a happily married woman."

"I won't," I speak through gritted teeth.

After he leaves, Max sits back on the sofa. "Everything all right?"

"Yep. Just trying to locate the dog."

As if beckoned, the dog comes barreling out of the kitchen. It runs around the couches and knocks into the coffee table, sending several small vases crashing to the floor, breaking into pieces, and finally leaps onto the pristine white couch, her claws ripping one of the seat cushions.

"No!" I yell, my skin prickling at the broken objects surrounding me. "Off, dog, er, Trixie. Off!"

She ignores me and licks my face, trying to sit her dense body on my narrow lap. Gently grasping her collar, Max pulls her off me and into a big embrace. The dog licks his face eagerly. "Hey, girl. I missed you too."

I look at the ruined sofa cushion and shattered vases, my ears growing hot. I pray the production's insurance will cover the damage. All the items are only borrowed from the designers. Flipping the cushion, I'm relieved there are no stains or tears on the other side. Taking the brush and shovel from the fireplace accoutrements, I sweep up the broken porcelain and dump them into one of the empty boxes, which still sits in the middle of the room.

The vases will need to be replaced before we shoot. I find a glass pitcher in one of the cupboards in the kitchen and take white hydrangeas from several vases around the living room and make a new arrangement. In the living room, Max is rolling around the floor with the dog, laughing like a schoolboy. I place the vase on the white acrylic coffee table.

"Wanna go for a walk, girl?" Max says to the now-calm dog sitting at his side.

At the word *walk*, the dog races to the front door and sits expectantly. Hmm, this rescue dog must have lived with a family at some point. Maybe we can pull this sleight of hand off. Putting on my white wool coat, I find the leash the kid left behind and clip it on the dog's collar. Before I can hand Max the leash, the dog shoots forward out the open front door. My body hits the side of the stone banister on the steps leading down to the sidewalk, and I stumble down after her,

51

trying to keep my feet under me, but I lose my balance and land flat on my stomach on the cold sidewalk, the leash escaping my grip. She's halfway down the street, nearing the church at the corner, when she rounds the bend toward the busier road, and my body freezes.

"Trixie, no!" I'm shouting. "Stop her!"

A flash of gray streaks past me as Max races after the dog. On my knees, I clamp my eyes shut and wait to hear tires screeching. Instead, hot breath and a large, wet tongue accost me. I relax.

"Don't do that, girl." My voice quivers. I take hold of the leash and scratch her head, the feel of the soft fur under my hands calming me. "Would you like to do the honors?" Without waiting for a reply, I hand the leash to Max, still shaking. It's early evening, but night has fully arrived. The moon is bright above, reflecting off the spattering of snow, lighting our path.

"That's strange. Trixie's never been this active. Her bones have been giving her trouble the past few years. But maybe I'm remembering wrong." Max is walking next to me toward the little garden overlooking the river and a cold wind whips around us from the icy waters. My body shivers, and I have a strong urge to snuggle into him. He exudes strength and confidence, and I want to wrap myself in it. The near accident still has me untethered.

"I was going to call her Holly after Holly Golightly from—"

"*Breakfast at Tiffany's,*" I finish. "Don't look so surprised. Every girl knows that movie."

"It was my mom's favorite," he says. My heart sinks, thinking of his parents. Poor Max. He must be lonely; he must need someone to—

"What the hell?!" Max shouts.

My mouth drops open as I see the dog lift up its leg and pee, his very male bits shimmering in the moonlight.

Oh, crap.

"I know I lost my memory for a couple of months, but I didn't lose my mind." His eyes narrow on my face. "What's going on?"

I rub my forehead, my brain running through excuses, until I say lightly, "Maybe some things are still jumbled in your mind." I quickly shuffle back to the brownstone.

Max runs after me, the dog barking and jumping happily beside him. "No. I remember my dog."

"I don't know. Maybe you should talk to your doctor. How would you know if you're forgetting something? You wouldn't." I'm going straight to hell. This guy was in a coma, has no parents, and I can't even tell him the truth about his dead dog.

Max places a hand on my arm. "I remember. And even if I didn't, I've seen pictures of her, and I know her name is Trixie. It's all over my Facebook page from a few years ago. My dog is a girl. It doesn't make sense." His face looks stricken, as if he's afraid he's lost something more than just his parents and his memory. "Where's your phone? I can look up my Facebook account."

God, now I really feel guilty.

"Please, don't worry too much about it." My hand squeezes his arm. "Talk to your aunt when she arrives. Maybe she can shine some light on it."

He considers this and then nods. His eyes fall to my hand, which still holds his arm. "It's funny, you don't seem like you're married," Max says, looking down at me. Bright headlights come up the street, and Max and I step apart.

"That must be the crew from *Wake Up*," I say, seeing a large black van and a slick Lincoln Town Car following close behind. "Do you mind finishing Trixie's walk without me? I need to get things ready."

I scurry back up the stairs to warn Natalie and Sam that the circus is about to begin.

Chapter 6

CATIE

Rushing into the townhouse, I yell Sam's and Natalie's names. I stop when I see Sam tucked inside the curtains of one of the tall windows in the living room looking out onto the street where I stood with Max. He slides his broad frame out, foam peanuts sticking to his cardigan sweater.

"What the hell are you wearing? You look like Mr. Rogers." I brush the foam pieces from his arms.

"I thought I'd get into the part of a married man and adoring husband."

"You look ridiculous." I begin to unbutton it.

"I'll do it." He throws it on a nearby chair. The light-blue button-down shirt he wears underneath brings out the specks of blue in his brown eyes. Around us, the room is clean and clear of the mess I created earlier. He must have cleaned while I was outside with Max. I smooth Sam's hair and kiss his cheek.

"Why'd you do that?" he asks.

"Thank you, Sam. You didn't have to do all this for me."

We smile at each other.

"Now don't fuck it up."

He frowns at my words, and I leave to find Natalie.

"They're here," I say, entering the kitchen. The fragrant smells from the many pots and pans bubbling on the stove make me pause. "This is heaven. What are we making tonight?"

Natalie tosses salt into a boiling pot and stirs vegetables sautéing in a cast iron skillet.

"Butternut risotto to start, lamb stew for the main, and individual apple tarts with hazelnut whipped cream to end."

My mouth is already watering. "You didn't have to do all this. The meal isn't even being filmed tonight."

"I couldn't help it. I wanted to start the weekend with a good impression."

"You're the best!" I say as the door chimes. "I'll post the menu on my next blog."

Did I imagine it, or did Natalie's hand falter as she stirred? Never once have I felt unwillingness on her part with our arrangement. She benefits from it as much as I do. And I never forced her into providing recipes. Then again, it was only meant to be a few recipes on my blog here and there, and now it's exploded into a whole brand. Soon, Natalie's going to open her own restaurant. Maybe she's having second thoughts about handing over her own creations. It's understandable, but what the hell will I do?

The doorbell chimes again.

Okay. Okay. I can't think about this now.

Back in the living room, I rush to Sam's side and put my arm in his as we open the door to Gillian talking loudly at Charles. Gillian's slim frame pushes into the foyer, her intimidating presence taking up the large space.

"What a horrible trip. The driver took us down every clogged street in Manhattan." She dumps her suitcases at my feet. "I'd call a helicopter for the trip home if I could."

Charles, David, the director, and a small crew follow Gillian inside. Giving instructions to a handful of other crew next to the van outside is Karen. I give her a wave.

"Spectacular," Gillian says, walking through the foyer into the living room. "Just as a *Simply Chic* home should look. And it smells delicious!"

Sam releases me, shoving his hand at Gillian. "Ms. Kennedy, I'm Samuel Harding. The managing editor for *Edge*."

"Very well." Gillian dismisses him, and I feel a sting as Sam's face falls. "Now where is the star of the show..."—I step forward—"my darling nephew, Maxie."

"He's outside walking Trixie." I make myself busy fixing drinks at the stocked wet bar in the corner. "Scotch? Beer?" Sam and Gillian each take a Scotch. Charles passes on a drink.

"I have to stay sharp," Charles explains.

There's a clamoring across the room. Trixie, or whatever his real name is, rushes past me, almost knocking the tray out of my hands. He bumps a side table in the formal sitting area, knocking over a stack of decorative books, and then disappears into the kitchen. I hear Natalie yelp and then a door slam.

"Young lady, you need to control that dog. We can't have her—" Gillian stops when she sees Max entering the room, his cheek's still flushed from the cold. As Gillian moves toward him, her lips press together, as if holding back emotion that wants to burst out of her. "Maxie. I'm so glad...you look...you're home." Her arms wrap around him, and his body tenses before relaxing, and he rests his chin on her shoulder.

I've never seen Gillian express so much raw emotion. I'd think it was for the cameras, except there aren't any.

"I'm sorry I didn't call." Max steps back.

"Don't even think about it." Gillian clears her throat, regaining her composure. "It's totally understandable. You've been through so much. It's time for you to relax and let someone else take care of you." Gillian scowls at me. Taking the cue, I offer Max a beer and escort him to one of the overstuffed Kathy Kuo regency armchairs in the formal sitting area across from the small settee where Sam sits.

"Give your uncle a hug." Gillian indicates Charles, who has been standing back, watching us. Taking notes for the taping most likely—*emotional reunion of aunt and beloved nephew*—except I don't think Max will want to be a performing monkey. *Wait? Did she just say uncle?*

"Mr. Friedman, you're related to Max?" I ask, surprised by this revelation. "Are you and Gillian siblings?"

"Married," he explains, as he leans in and hugs Max. It's one of those manly hugs where their hands clasp in the middle, so there is minimal body contact. They slap each other on the back to indicate the hug is over.

Charles, Gillian, and Max dive into small talk, and I deposit the empty tray on the bar and discreetly throw back two fingers of Scotch. There were a couple of moments in the meeting in Gillian's office that made me think Charles and she had worked together before, but I haven't seen an ounce of affection between them. Then again, Gillian has never seemed like the warm-and-fuzzy type.

"What happened to Trixie?" Max directs his question at Gillian and Charles.

I almost spit out the scotch in my mouth.

"What do you mean? You just saw her."

"That's not Trixie," Max presses. "That dog is a boy."

"What?!" Gillian wrings her hands and shoots dagger eyes at me. As if I had anything to do with the dog. I've got too many other spinning plates to juggle than to be part of this dog charade. A chuckle escapes Charles's lips, and he quickly sucks his cheeks in, holding back a laugh when Gillian shoots a sharp look at him.

"Perhaps you're still having some issues with your memory?" Gillian offers, but she isn't convincing. Her eyes dance around the room and won't focus on anyone.

"Don't bother, Gilli. The last thing Max needs is to think he really has lost his mind." Charles gives Max's shoulder a soft squeeze. "Trixie died."

"Please don't be upset," Gillian entreats, rubbing vigorously at an invisible stain on her houndstooth skirt. "Trixie passed away last month from bone cancer, and after everything you've been through, we"—Charles clears his throat loudly—"*I* didn't want you to have to deal with another loss." She grabs his hands, her eyes pleading with him to forgive her. It seems to work, and his stiff back softens back into the armchair.

"Whose dog is that?"

"I searched the shelters until I found the perfect greyhound to bring home for you. His name's Bailey. Doesn't he look just like Trixie?" Gillian acts as if this was an act of endearment and not a sleight of hand she wasn't meant to be caught in.

Max shrugs, and I can see the fight leave him, as if he doesn't have the energy to berate his aunt.

Behind me, I feel someone staring and find a camera pointed at me. Dabbing my mouth, I smile widely and sit next to Sam on the settee.

"Hey, what are you doing?" Sam turns his head away from the camera. In order for this ploy to work, Sam can't be filmed. At least, not from the front. I spoke to Karen about it last week, and she barely batted an eye when I told her Sam only wanted to be shot from behind or in distant background shots. Sam was right—they really only care about capturing moments with Max Euston in Catelyn Bloom's picture-perfect home life.

Max glances at us and I smile, talking quietly through my teeth. "I know. I'll talk to Charles."

"This isn't a joke to me, Catie. Fix it." Sam leaves in a huff, playing the perfect part of the disgruntled husband.

"Everything all right?" Max moves next to me.

"Yep. Great!" I squeak. "Could I have a word with you, Mr. Friedman?"

"What's the problem?" Gillian narrows her eyes.

"Oh, uh…it's just that Sam's a private person, and we agreed he wouldn't be filmed from the front."

"Don't worry, these are just test shots," Charles assures me and turns back to Gillian, continuing their conversation.

I'm not convinced, but I leave it and turn to Max. "It must be a change coming from…uh, where were you?"

"Greece. I was in a hospital there for several months, though I was only conscious the last few weeks." Max looks at his feet.

"Will you go back?" I ask.

"No. I finished the piece I was working on when…when I got injured." His voice has turned gravelly. "Can we talk about something else? I was hoping this would also be a holiday away from all that."

"Of course."

David, wearing black pants, a black turtleneck, and holding an iPad, comes up to Charles and whispers something into his ear.

"Excuse me, Ms. Bloom, but I have to go deal with some things for tomorrow. Karen has the updated shot list, and she can fill you in."

Sam has come into the room and sits next to me. "Did you fix it?"

"They're not even filming right now," I whisper.

"Dinner is almost ready!" Natalie sticks her head out from the kitchen.

"Who was that?" Gillian points accusing eyes at the swinging door Natalie has disappeared behind. "Why aren't you cooking the meal?"

"I did! I mean I prepared the menu, but my sister Natalie is helping with the cooking tonight."

Oh, crap. Gillian looks really mad.

"It's not the same. Send her away and get in the kitchen. Catelyn Bloom should be doing all the cooking this weekend. Not some second-rate hack."

My cheeks burn in anger. I want to defend Natalie, but I can't. And I can't go in the kitchen. My cover would be blown. Natalie and I have practiced the homecoming-dinner menu, but not tonight's meal. There is no reason for me to be cooking tonight. That wasn't discussed in any of the meetings.

"My wife is exhausted and has a full day tomorrow with the breakfast and dinner and all the preparations she's handled leading up to this shoot. She needs the night off," Sam jumps in, gently caressing my shoulder. "Besides, they're not even filming this meal."

"Unacceptable. I expect every meal this weekend to be prepared by Catelyn Bloom."

"Trust me, it'll be much better," Sam mutters, and I pinch his arm.

Gillian is staring at me with her steel-gray eyes.

"Really, you won't even notice. I taught my sister everything she knows."

Gillian is an unmoving rock. I wish there was a cliff I could kick her off. "Go finish the dinner. I don't want second best. And neither does Max."

Before I can respond, Sam steps close to Gillian.

"My wife's exhausted, and we all have a big day tomorrow. There is no reason for her to be cooking tonight. If you want to blame someone, blame me. It was my idea that she take the night off."

Gillian's lips purse, and she looks from Sam to me.

"You don't want her to have a nervous breakdown and have to cancel the whole special entirely, do you?" Sam is speaking in a low, firm voice.

Gillian relents. "Fine, fine. But I expect her to prepare tomorrow's meal from beginning to end. Everything must run perfectly, with you at the center."

"I wouldn't have it any other way," I say as I escort us all into the formal dining room for dinner.

I don't know why Gillian is making such a fuss about the food tonight. We could just have easily ordered takeout. Until two weeks ago, she'd never shown any interest in me or my cooking, other than her pleasure with the increased readership since I began writing for her magazine. She's up to something. This weekend is about more than just a reunion with her nephew. But I don't know what, yet, and I'm not sure I want to find out.

Chapter 7
NATALIE

Dumping the pumpkin puree, sour cream, eggs, and spices into the stainless steel mixer, I flick it on, watching the ingredients move back and forth until they are creamy and fragrant. It was a long day of cooking and serving the evening meal, and I still have the whole meal to prep for the filming of tomorrow's breakfast and homecoming feast.

After the meal, the dishes were washed and put in the dishwasher (thanks to Sam and Max—Catie was off at some production meeting), and I was able to sleep for a few hours, setting my alarm for eleven, hoping everyone would be settled into their rooms by then.

The puree pours easily into the two graham cracker piecrusts I made earlier, but a sound from the living room makes me pause. Creeping across the room, I put my ear on the swinging door and yelp when it flings open toward my head. Max's face, on the other side of the door, reflects my surprise.

"I thought everyone was asleep." I stay in the doorway, blocking his view.

"Nightcap," Max explains, holding up a bottle of Macallan 18. "But I can't find a glass on the wet bar."

"Go sit down on the sofa, and I'll bring you a glass. They were all used during cocktail hour." He doesn't budge. "It looks so cozy by the fire," I urge.

"Grab a glass, and join me."

"I can't. Too much to do."

"What do you mean?"

"Uh, nothing. I mean, it's late."

"Something smells amazing in here."

Pushing his way in, I cringe at the mess behind me, the uncooked cheesecakes still sitting on the counter next to the stove. "You just missed Catie," I say as an explanation.

"Isn't Catie doing all the cooking on camera?" Max sits at the butcher-block island, the whiskey bottle standing firmly on the counter in front of him. Holding back a groan, I slide him a glass. A very small glass. He fills it to the brim, drinks it, and fills it again.

"They're shooting her making the soup, sides, and turkey for the special. They'll have a shot of the cakes after they're made and post the recipe online."

"It's sounds like she's cooking a Thanksgiving meal."

"Your aunt said that you loved all the food she made for you every Thanksgiving, so I...er...I mean, Catie thought it would be nice to make a similar meal for you."

"My aunt never cooks." Max laughs. "But she did have an amazing catering service every year. And I did love it."

"You don't think Catie will mind me raiding her liquor cabinet?" Max asks, turning the bottle around in his hand.

"It's not really her house. I thought Catie told you."

"She did. I keep forgetting."

From the news coverage I've seen, Max went through quite an ordeal in Greece, but I wonder if his memory is back to normal. It was all for a great reason. He saved that little girl.

"Those look good. Can I have a taste?"

I swipe the cheesecakes from the counter and place them in the hot oven. "They're not ready."

"Why isn't Catie making the cakes?"

"Oh, um…she whipped the ingredients up earlier, and I told her I'd bake them for her."

Max eyes the freshly used mixer and open egg carton.

"And clean up."

There's not much to clean, just a couple of large bowls, teaspoons, and the beaters. I dump them into the sink, do a quick rinse, and wipe down the counter.

"I'm about done here."

I flick off the recessed lighting.

"Don't you have to wait until the cheesecakes are cooked?"

Damn. I was hoping he wouldn't notice that little detail and leave. There is still the praline topping for the cheesecakes to make, the ingredients for the stuffing, and seasoning for the turkey to prepare, and the bacon-and-leek soup to prep before I can go back to bed. And none of it can be done with him watching.

"Oh, right." I snap the lights back on, pour a whiskey, and lean against the counter, staring Max down.

The whiskey slowly seeps into my bloodstream, making my already-exhausted body deflate a little more. Too bad he isn't a Tequila drinker. That always perks me up—and makes me do crazy things. Even crazier than getting up in the middle of the night to do enough prep work so my sister can fake making an entire feast tomorrow.

"I think everyone's gone to bed." I yawn to make my point.

As Max drains his glass, I relax. Good, he's done. Then he fills it back up.

"I have a few things I have to do, so…"

"I'll just sit over here and read." At the breakfast nook, Max opens *The New York Times.*

"That's not exactly what I meant."

Checking the oven, I see that the cheesecakes are beginning to set, but they still have at least thirty minutes. Frustration is building, but I don't want to be rude to the guest of honor, so I resort to crossing my arms and staring at Max as he pretends to read. I know he's not reading, because his eyes are staring at one spot on the page, unmoving.

"You can go to bed." Max keeps his eyes on the paper. "I can take the cakes out when the buzzer rings and put them in the fridge or wherever."

Like I'd ever leave it to a timer. This is an unfamiliar oven. I have no idea if it cooks hot or cool or which rack is ideal for baking. It's a science, and I'm the scientist. I have to keep a close watch on them in this new environment.

"I forget how long they're meant to cook, so I better keep checking them until they're done." I force a laugh. "Catie is much better at this than me."

A moment passes.

"I don't bite. Sit down. Fill up your glass." Max kicks the chair out next to him.

"I'd rather stay by the oven."

Finishing the glass of whiskey, I slam it on the counter louder than I meant to.

"Have I done something to offend you?"

"I just like to be alone when I..."—the word *cook* almost escapes my lips—"at night."

"I don't." He snaps the paper open in his hands. "I hate being alone. Especially at night."

The words drop an idea into my head, and I grab my phone.

Folding the newspaper down, Max watches me, but I turn my body away and scroll down my phone. "It must take real talent to create something like that." Max indicates the cakes in the oven.

"Our mother is the true genius. She could give Julia Child a run for her money," I babble as I tap out a text to Catie. "After our father died, Mom would do whatever it took to keep her mind busy. Cooking became her drug of choice. But she loved it too. I spent most of my adolescence in the kitchen with her and my grandmother. It was my own escape. It still is."

"Is your mother...er...still..."

"Huh? Oh, yeah, yeah. She's alive. She just spends most her time with her new husband, jet-setting between their homes in Panama and South Florida." Not really aware of what's coming out of my mouth, I glare at my phone, but no reply has come.

"When did you lose your father?"

"When I was twelve." Still no response. "I'll be right—"

"I lost my parents when I was thirteen."

I can't skip out of the conversation now. He's opening up to me, and I'm busy trying to save my own hide. Who knows the last time he's been able to really talk to someone. He was without his memory for two months, and when he got it back, he was surrounded by strangers, as far as I've read.

"How did they..." Why can no one ever just say the word die?

"A semitruck smashed into my dad's car. The driver had been driving all night and fell asleep at the wheel."

"Wow. That's horrible. I'm sorry." I lean back on the counter, forgetting my mission for a moment. "You must hate him."

"The driver died too. And he left behind a toddler, a little girl named Lily. It was horrible for everyone involved. I still keep in touch with the little girl. She's twenty-three now."

"Where does she live?"

"Allentown, Pennsylvania. Near where I grew up."

"My mom says I was really depressed when my dad died," I reveal.

It's been a while since I've thought about my dad or when he was sick. My most vivid memory is feeling an intense need to protect Catie. She was ten when he finally passed away, after two years in and out of the hospital with pancreatic cancer (which Catie thought was called pancake cancer, and she still won't touch pancakes). My mom was such a wreck at the hospital when he died. I wanted to be the one to tell Catie. I didn't want Mamé to tell her. She would have dropped it like a piece of plywood on Catie's head. No tenderness. Just—*clunk!*—your dad is dead. When Mamé took me home to get some things for Mom, I raced to my sister's room and locked the door. She was inside reading, and I could hear the low rumbling of voices below and a door closing as Mamé relieved our neighbor from her babysitting duties.

I made Catie put the book down and told her I had very serious news that was going to be upsetting, and we were both going to have to be grown-ups about it. I said she could cry if she wanted but not in front of Mom or Mamé. It would upset them too much. After I told her, she nodded her head and looked at me with solemn eyes and asked if she could wear her pink dress to the funeral. It was our daddy's favorite. Then she went back to her book.

At the funeral, Catie wore her pink dress, and I stood by her, ready to pounce on anyone who said anything mean about it, but no one did. Everyone thought it was sweet. There were a lot of tears at the funeral from friends and acquaintances watching the two sweet daughters of the man who had died. Being the center of attention made me feel uncomfortable, but Catie smiled chastely at all the attention and let the guests coddle her.

"All I remember is wanting to protect Catie from the pain and shock I felt when Mom said he was gone. I don't remember being depressed. I made it my mission to keep Catie happy and shield her from Mom's and our mamé's grief. But I can't look at pictures or videos of Dad and me together. You'd think I'd want to look at them all the time, but it makes me feel sick. My subconscious must be holding on to the loss. But day to day, it's not something that I think much about anymore."

"That was one of the great side effects of amnesia. I forgot all the pain in my life. I had to live in the moment. I couldn't even think about my future because I didn't know what I wanted it to be. My memories coming back were a blessing and a curse."

I smile and squeeze Max's hand. "That's one of the sweetest and saddest things I've ever heard."

He smiles back, and I reluctantly take my hand away. I want to know more about this man and what made him take the heroic leap to rescue that kidnapped girl, but the clock is ticking, and I can't afford to be a zombie tomorrow. After checking the cakes, I look at the time. It's almost midnight. I have to finish the prep and if Max isn't leaving, I need Catie.

"I'll be right back."

"Where's Bailey?" Max calls to me as I take the back stairs two by two.

"Sleeping in the laundry room." I hold back a yelp as I crash into Catie at the top of the stairs.

"Did you get my text?" I demand. "You have to come downstairs."

"I'm exhausted. I just got out of a two-hour production meeting, which was meant to be fifteen minutes, but no one could decide anything, and get this, now they want to film the interview and the party at some historic hotel in Downtown Brooklyn. They are insisting it will be the picture-perfect end to this nightmare of a farce, and they want us all to attend."

"We have bigger problems. Get out your magic spatula—we have to perform a little sleight of hand."

"What are you talking about?" Catie raises an eyebrow, a look she perfected in her childhood, practicing in the mirror when she thought nobody was watching.

"Max is hanging around the kitchen and won't leave. You have to come down and help me finish the prep." This should be enough to convince Catie, but she still looks dubious. "There won't be time to do it in the morning, and if I don't get this meal to a place where you can just dump stuff together and stick it in the oven tomorrow, you'll be screwed. Unless you want to learn how to cook a turkey, whip together the bacon-and-leek soup, and make the praline topping from scratch?"

"Okay, okay, but won't Max notice that you're doing all the work?"

"Keep your phone on you. I've got a plan."

Back in the kitchen, Max is still nestled into the breakfast nook, the dog snuggled next to him. I pull out all the ingredients we need and lay them out on the island.

"Hi, Max," Catie trills, smiling sweetly.

He smiles widely back.

I shove the bag of almonds into Catie's hands. "You make the praline topping. I'll get started on the soup."

"Are you crazy," Catie hisses. "I burned it three times when we tried to do it in the test kitchen."

"Maybe the fourth time's a charm," I hiss back. Pulling my chef's knife out of its holder, I swiftly chop the onions and garlic for the stuffing.

"Damn, you're fast. Aren't you worried about chopping off a finger?"

The voice startles me. Max is hunched over the island watching us, the dog sniffing around the counter. Maybe I should slow down, try to look more like an amateur, but it's nearly impossible. I've been doing this for too long.

"We all have a talent for something. My knife-handling skills have always been fierce. Too bad my cooking skills don't match up."

Beside the stove, Max moves next to Catie, who is staring at the sugar, almonds, butter, vanilla, and saucepan on the counter in front of her. I cringe as Catie brings the knife down on the almonds, causing several of them to fly off the cutting board, the dog hungrily eating them up.

"Sorry." Catie grins at Max. "I'm a bit tired."

"Understandably. You've got a lot going on. Can I help?"

"Have you ever chopped almonds?"

"I've hardly chopped anything."

Taking his hand in hers, she places it on the knife, and they slowly slice the almonds.

"See, it's not that hard."

"Catie the sugar!" I yell as dark smoke rises from the pot.

Forgoing the almonds, Catie shoves the pot off the burner, but it's too late. The sugar is burned.

"Sorry, I was a little distracted." Catie shoots Max a coquettish smile.

For God's sake, does my sister have to be so obvious? And she's meant to be married! Shoving Catie and Max out of the way, I chop the almonds into a fine dust and heat another small pot on the stove.

"I've got this, Nat." Catie nudges me away. "Why don't you finish chopping the leeks and onions for the soup."

Ignoring Catie's condescending tone, I let her take control—or appear to—watching Catie out of the corner of my eye as I put the chopped ingredients into Tupperware containers so everything is *mise en place* for tomorrow. Ten minutes later, the praline is almost done—thankfully, nothing is burned this time—and will need to be spread out onto wax paper soon, but I hold back instructions, letting Catie sweat it out for a bit.

"Do you cook, Max?" Catie asks, casually stirring.

Slicing easily through the onions, oranges, and lemons for the turkey, I put them aside, reaching for the rosemary and thyme.

"I can boil up a mean pot of water." Max leans against the counter. "Traveling for a living and staying in hotel rooms isn't ideal for cooking."

My phone vibrates. A message from Catie.

Now what??

Spread it onto wax paper.

Where?

In pantry?

Where's pantry?

"Are you kidding me?" I say out loud.

"What?" Max asks.

"Nothing." I make a point of banging the walk-in pantry door open. "Just forgot something in the *pantry*." Dumping the wax paper on the counter, I pick the leaves off the herb stems, readying it to be stuffed in the turkey cavity for tomorrow.

"No!" I scream suddenly as I watch Catie pour the entire praline mixture into a glob on the wax paper. Catie freezes.

Max is staring at us. If he has any sense something is amiss, he isn't showing it. He looks amused, not suspicious.

When the dog starts barking by the back door, I jump on the opportunity to get Max out of the house. "Do you mind taking her out?"

"Him," Catie says. "The dog is a he."

"What are you talking about?"

"Gillian told Max what really happened to his dog."

"Okay. Fine. Whatever. Can you take *him* for a walk?"

71

Catie mentioned something about the real dog dying and having to foster a look-alike, but I'd forgotten until now. I'm glad he knows. It's one less lie to remember.

When Max is gone, I throw the (second!) ruined praline concoction away and send Catie to fetch the turkey from the smaller fridge in the pantry.

"Just stuff all this inside the cavity and brush the olive oil and garlic over the skin." I shove the cutting board of ingredients at Catie.

"Don't I need to do all this tomorrow on camera?" Catie asks.

"Oh, right. Shoot. Never mind. Put all the ingredients in separate containers and place them in the fridge."

As Catie organizes the ingredients, I quickly caramelize another batch of sugar and chop more almonds. By the time Max returns, the new batch is spread evenly over the wax paper, and the turkey ingredients are prepped and put away.

"Everything looks good here," Catie says brightly. "If you can handle the rest—"

Before she can finish the statement, the dog, full of energy from his walk, comes bounding around the counter and leaps up, grabbing the turkey between his jaws, dragging it across the floor.

"The turkey!"

Catie and I chase after the dog as he drags the raw turkey across the kitchen floor and into the laundry room. Catie reaches out, but the dog growls at her, and she snatches her hand back.

"You get it," Catie insists.

"I'm not going near that animal."

The dog starts to chew one of the legs, and I yell, "Stop!" But he ignores me and sinks his teeth in deeper. The sound of a box of food shaking behind me draws the dog's attention, and he leaps past us and back into the kitchen.

Looking at the sad carcass in front of me, I tell Catie to grab the mangled bird.

"Gross. I'm not touching that thing."

"Catie!" I've had enough of my sister's prissy attitude for the night.

Trudging toward the bird, Catie attempts to grip one of its legs between her fingers, but it slides out. Looking around the kitchen, she takes a towel from the shelf behind her and wraps the turkey in it, carrying it back to the kitchen and dumping it in the sink.

"Can it be saved?" Catie wonders allowed.

Looking it over, I see one of the legs hanging on by a thin tendon. "I can pin it together I think, and we can angle this section away from the camera. It's gonna need a good scrub though."

The dog barks, and I protectively cover the turkey. "What did you give him?" I ask Max.

"I found some bacon bits in the cupboard." Max smiles, scratching the content dog behind the ears.

Placing the rinsed turkey in the roasting pan, Catie vigorously washes her hands and dries them. "I need to go talk to Sam about tomorrow before he goes to bed."

After Catie leaves, Max sits at the table, the dog resting at his feet. "What do you do for a living?"

"I'm Catie's manager," I answer automatically as I open drawers, trying to find something to pin the leg back together with.

What's another lie on top of so many.

"Do you smell that?"

"Oh, no! The cakes!" I throw the oven door open and my face crumbles. The tops are black. "They're ruined."

After I dump the mess into the trash, I slide down the cupboards and bury my face in my knees, the last bit of energy leached from my body.

"Do you want me to get Catie?"

"No!" I bark at Max hovering above me. "She'll only make it worse."

Screw it. Catie can make them tomorrow. If I e-mail her the recipe to study, Catie could do it. It's not that hard. Except Catie will ruin it. I know she will.

"Let me help you."

"Can't you just leave me alone?!" I immediately regret my outburst, but I'm exhausted and frustrated, and I just want him to leave so I can to finish the baking and fall into bed before the craziness begins tomorrow.

There's hurt behind Max's words as he speaks, "Sorry. I'll get out of your hair."

Before he can leave, Catie enters again from the back stairs, looking between Max and me. "Is everything all right?"

"Fine," I assert. "I thought you were going to bed?"

"Sam's trapped Gillian in our room, talking her through his latest idea for some new sports features." Catie turns her attention to Max. "Natalie's not keeping you up is she? She loves to talk."

"I was just heading up to bed."

"I'll escort you." Catie puts her hand on Max's arm and pulls him out the swinging door into the living room. "I hate walking through a dark house alone."

When they're gone, I throw cool water on my face, turn to the pantry, and take out the ingredients for the cheesecakes, placing them on the counter. Then I pull out two frozen piecrusts. It's a last-minute save, and I hate using anything that isn't from scratch, but I'm too tired and angry to care.

In the silence, I realize I was enjoying Max's company, but, yet again, Catie swept in and took the one bit of light from my day and made it her own. For the first time since we began this sham, I'm beginning to wonder what I'm doing here. I'm about to open my own business, and I want to expand it into more than a restaurant. I want to be a brand, with gourmet products and cookbooks that make the bestseller charts—but with *my* name on it. I don't want to be shoved in a kitchen, pretending to be Catelyn Bloom's lowly assistant.

Something has to change. Soon.

Chapter 8
CATIE

"It must be hard work." Max hands me a tumbler from the cabinet under the wet bar where we found some extra glasses, and he pours whiskey halfway up the small glass. "Being the star of a TV show, all the prep for this shoot, and hosting all of us...it can't be easy."

A star. I like that.

"I'm hardly a star," I say instead. The whiskey heats my throat on the way down and warms my body, and for the first time all day, I relax. "Don't be fooled; the glamorous life of TV isn't so glamorous."

And after this weekend, I may have to give it up. Rushing around the kitchen tonight sent my pulse racing. How the hell am I going to pull this off with a camera crew on all sides of me? I barely pulled it off in front of one man tonight.

The set of *Wake Up, America!* is a well-oiled machine. But "on location"—as this is referred to—there is a lot more planning, and things change by the minute. Charles kept me upstairs with the crew for two hours as he went through every shot for tomorrow, which led to more back-and-forths with Karen, mainly about the interview with Max. The morning host from *Wake Up* who was going to conduct the interview can't do it now, so they had to change the format. They've made me the interviewer instead. I can see it now: *Catelyn Bloom's Special Homecoming Interview with Max Euston...Only on* Wake Up, America!

What a tangled web I've woven.

"It's going to be a long day tomorrow. I should head up." On top of everything, being close to Max makes my head spin and makes me want to say and do things that will put us all in jeopardy.

Before I can turn away, Max asks, "Aren't you going to put out the fire?"

Staring at the burning cinders, I look at the tools next to it. I grab the poker.

"The shovel might be better."

Quickly, I put the poker back and take the shovel, holding it out to Max. "You do it."

As he smothers the burning cinders, I walk through the room, turning off the table lamps and fluffing pillows, repositioning throws that have been bunched and fallen off sofas.

"You hate turning off the lights at night." Max states this fact as if we've known each other for years.

"How did you...oh, my blog. I forgot I mentioned that. Yes, I hate to admit it, but I'm afraid of the dark."

Max turns off the last light and leads me to the staircase, his hand firm on my back. "I'll help you with the rest."

At the top landing, we work our way down the narrow hallway, until all the lights have been extinguished.

"This is me," I say, leaning against the wall outside the master suite. It's dark, but I can feel Max, all manly and warm, close by.

"You're not what I expected," he says.

"What did you expect?"

"Someone old and stodgy. But you're young, vibrant, and sexy as hell."

"Watch it, young man. I'm a married woman." But I don't move.

His hand slides around the back of my waist, kneading the skin as electric shocks shoot into me, warming my insides. Before I can pucker my lips, the door across the hall bangs open and light spills over us. Surprise turns quickly to anger on Sam's face as he spots us.

"Hi, honey." I move swiftly to him, and Max's hand falls away. "Max was just helping me turn off the lights. You know how I'm scared of the dark."

I'm ready for Sam to lunge at the poor guy when he yanks me inside the room, slamming the door. Without a word, Sam goes into the bathroom, kicking the door shut. I can't really blame him for being pissed. From now on, I've really got to keep my libido in check. Kissing Max is not something happily married women do. I must remember that. But it's not like we're really married, right?

It's been an exhausting day, and all I want to do is go to bed, except all my toiletries are in the bathroom. How long does it take for a man to shower? Geez. When the water finally stops running, I bang on the door.

It flies open. Sam has his hand on the frame, scowling at me. My eyes fall to the towel wrapped around his waist and then to his muscled abs and the little trail of hair below his belly button.

Chill. This is Sam. I already knew he was fit and hot and perfect. Physically.

"I can wait." I swallow.

"No, please come in. Make yourself at home."

"You're in a mood," I bristle, grabbing my toothbrush from my pile of toiletries spread chaotically across the bathroom counter.

"Am I? Well, I did just catch my *wife* almost kissing another man." Sam uses a small towel to roughly dry his hair, his chest muscles flexing as he does this. This isn't the first time I've seen Sam without a shirt on—in the mornings at work, he often does a quick change from the previous day's shirt. See? Total scoundrel—but being this close to his half-naked body is visceral. I'm having a biological reaction to the intimate act of getting ready for bed together, and the steam of the shower and smell of soap and aftershave are not helping matters.

"Oh, please. You're getting a little too into the role playing." I scrub vigorously at my teeth.

"This isn't a game, Catie. This is my life." Sam whips off his towel.

Do not look down.

But I do. It's quick. Just a snap of my eyes, but I see him. All of him. And I shove my toothbrush back in my mouth, stifling a moan. My cheeks are flushing bright red. Finally, he puts his boxers on. But they're short and tight. I keep my eyes firmly on his face, focusing on the fight. The fight will keep my mind off it…er, him.

"I know that," I manage. "It's my life too."

"No, it's not just your life. It's your sister's, and Patrick's, and mine. How can you be so selfish and almost ruin everything for a stupid kiss?!" He spins the top off the mouthwash, takes a swig, and spits it out. "If you want to be kissed, I can kiss you."

"Don't start that." Except I kinda want him to start that. Damn whiskey. "Besides, I think I really like Max."

Sam wipes his mouth roughly with the back of his hand. "You barely know him. And it doesn't matter. You can't go there. Ever!"

He storms out of the bathroom. I follow him. Pacing the floor, he sets his face all hard and serious. It's damn sexy.

Get a grip, girl. I've always known he's hot. It's just all this pretending. It's got me confused. *He's a player,* I remind myself. Once he has me, he'll toss me away. Do not be a sucker. Do not let your heart go there.

Suddenly he turns on me. "You know what? This is over. I'm telling Gillian in the morning."

"No! Sam, I'm sorry."

He stops abruptly, causing me to slam into his back. When he turns, his face burns into mine. "You're obviously not taking this seriously," he accuses. "Why should I?"

"You promised." The whine in my voice disturbs me. "Why are you being like this? If I didn't know better, I'd say you're jealous."

Sam rakes his hands through his hair, his face steaming. "Everyone is turning their lives inside out for you. I have given you a husband, *everything* so you won't lose your job. Natalie is working her ass off and getting no credit from anyone, including you, and Patrick has been lying for you for years, and now you're willing to throw it all away for some fling?"

Heat shoots up my neck. "You volunteered to do this. I didn't force you. And Natalie's a big girl. Hell, this was her idea. And Patrick...well, you're right about Patrick; he didn't sign up for any of this. But he never told me to stop either." I'm right in Sam's face, unfaltering. "Who cares if I kiss Max? He wanted to kiss me. I mean, I know you play at liking me, but it's always just been a game."

Sam is fidgeting and avoiding my eyes. Suddenly he doesn't look angry—he looks vulnerable. And scared.

Oh. My. God.

"You can't like me," I say in dismay.

He shoves past me.

"Even if you think you do, it's a lie. You go out with a different woman every week. Every day! You're a total player."

Sam explodes. "Because I can't have the one girl I really want! I know you think I've been asking you out for *four years* so I can tick off some notch on my belt, and I've let you think that. Because if you really knew…if you knew the truth…"

My hands are covering my gaping mouth.

"Please tell me this isn't some ploy to get me to sleep with you," I finally manage.

"Of course, I want to sleep with you! I'm in love with you!"

Oh my God. He means it. I think he means it.

"You can't be in love with me. You hardly know me. Not really."

"I know you." His voice is low.

"What are my favorite books?" I challenge. "Movies? Where do I like to vacation? The name of my first boyfriend? Where did I grow up? Go to college?"

When he looks up, his expression is guarded. "Those are just facts."

"No, they're what a friend would know about me. And especially someone who loves me."

"Fine. I'll play your game." He crosses his arms, stepping closer. "I know your favorite color is pink, though you say it's Tiffany Blue. You say you're from Boston, but you're really from a small town fifty miles outside of it. You favor salty to sweet. Your favorite book is *Gone with the Wind*, but you hated the sequel. You won't give money to the homeless because you don't want them to buy drugs or alcohol, but you will give them a Subway or Starbucks gift card, which you usually have ready in your wallet. And you say no to me because you're afraid I'm not serious, and you'll get hurt or look like a fool, even though I'm the fool who's been asking you out every week for four years and has been rejected every time."

I'm so caught up in his version of me—much more accurate than I want to admit—that I am almost out of my body, floating above the scene. When I slip back into it, tears are running down my face. I swipe at them with my sleeve.

"I had no idea. You never seemed serious." I blink, recovering. "And you do always have a new girl on your arm. And when I met you, you did that awful thing to Beth. How could I have known?"

Sam yanks his track pants and shoes out of his suitcase. "It doesn't matter now because you're right. I don't know you. Everything you've shown me in the last twelve hours is not who I thought you were." He pulls his pants on and stuffs his feet in his shoes. "I'll play along with your little hoax—for Patrick's sake—but when we get back to the city, I don't want to see you anymore." Yanking the door open he says, "Don't wait up."

Before he exits, he looks back at me; my face is distorted from everything I'm still processing from his confession. For a moment, I think he'll rush to me and sweep me up into a long embrace, but he gives a slow shake of his head and says, "This is over."

How can this be over?! I want to yell. I didn't even realize it had begun.

Chapter 9
NATALIE

Sleep doesn't come naturally to me. There was an article recently that listed ways to get a better night's sleep. I tried to follow the list of dos and don'ts, but most of the suggestions on the list stressed me out more than they helped:

1. Don't drink alcohol after 6 p.m. (Ha! How else am I going to relax?)
2. An hour before bed, turn off all technology. (FOMO can make this very stressful.)
3. Put on Mozart. (Easy.)
4. Write all anxieties or worries into a notebook. (But what if someone finds it and reads it?!)
5. Don't call or talk to my sister before bed. (This was my own rule, and if I followed rule number two, I wouldn't need rule number five.)

Last night, I broke every rule.

All I've been thinking about is Catie and our arrangement. Hey, I know the deal with my sister is two sided. Catie never forced me to hand over the recipes. Hell, it had been my idea. Just like showing up and doing all the work for this TV special was my idea. But Catie knew all she had to do was tell me her predicament and I would come to the rescue. It's always been this way.

Even though I'm two years older than my sister, I always looked up to Catie as a kind of superhero: beautiful, articulate, desired by the opposite (and same) sex, stylish, and clever. The typical adored youngest child. And after our father died, I made sure everything continued to come easy to her. I thought I was protecting her, but maybe I've been enabling her all along.

From an early age, I new Catie was special. All the kids in our neighborhood chased after Catie's friendship, and I was accepted only because I was cool little Catie Bloom's sister. And Catie was always thrown into my activities because our mother worked full time for a catering company and didn't have time to cart both of us to separate activities every day, so Catie ended up being stuck in whatever I was interested in, at first. And then it slowly shifted, and I was suddenly only involved in the activities Catie loved—swimming, drama, dance. It was only natural that I was compared to Catie. We're sisters. When Catie started wearing baby doll dresses and Mary Janes, I was right there with her. Being the older sister, I should have been setting the trends, but I wasn't risky enough. I always liked to blend in, especially during my adolescence. Catie loved to stand out.

When I started high school, Catie still had two years left at the middle school, and I finally found my own interests. By then I knew I loved cooking from helping my mother and Mamé in the kitchen. Catie stuck her nose up at my efforts in the kitchen, calling me a "Momma's girl."

On the first day of school my freshman year, I tried out for track with a friend who was scared to do it on her own, and I realized I had a knack for sprinting. It was tasking, tearing over the asphalt, fast and hard, my legs burning, but I was good at it. And I loved it because there was always an end in sight. A clear finish line.

When I first volunteered the recipes to help Catie with her fledgling blog, I saw the finish line. But when Catie was offered the book deal and promised me half the profits, I jumped at it, happily pushing that line back myself. As Catie's career exploded, the line faded, until I could no longer see an end.

After last night, I feel lost and unsure of how to move forward with my sister. The extra income from Catie's book has given me the seed money I need to open my own restaurant, which has been my dream all along. And I hope to publish several cookbooks once I've settled into my new business. The only way I'm ever going to make this dream into a reality is to get out of this tangled web of deception.

When I woke up from my restless sleep this morning, my whole body screamed at me to move my feet and go for a run to clear my head of this mess I've created in my life. Running always helps my subconscious mind solve problems my conscious mind is too muddled to see through. No matter where I travel, I always bring my running shoes.

Leaning against the closed laundry room door in the kitchen, I pull my right ankle up to stretch my thigh. When I shift to the other foot, the door suddenly gives way, and I tumble forward, landing on something hard. Rolling off, I discover Sam sleeping on the floor under a fleece blanket, Bailey curled up at his feet.

His body shifts, and I roll onto the cold tiles.

"What are you doing here?" His voice is thick with sleep.

"What are *you* doing here?" I shoot back.

Sam gives me a look that says *take one guess* and sits up. Bailey leaps to his feet, barking and bouncing around the small room, causing us to slam into the door, the wall, and

BROOKE STANTON

each other. When I finally pull the door open, the dog dashes to the back door, scratching maniacally at the frame.

Sam pushes the door open, and the dog bursts out.

"I thought you were afraid of the dog?"

"Me too, but when I was lying on the floor, pissed off and feeling sorry for myself, in came Bailey, and he curled up next to me. How could I resist such a sweet bedfellow? Plus, he's a very nice heater."

"Did you go for a run?" I ask, taking in his sneakers, track pants, and hoodie.

"Late last night. I needed to let off some steam. You?"

"I'm just going for a short jog to clear my head before the curtain goes up."

"I'll come with you. I still have some hot air to release."

Sam calls Bailey in from the back, and he follows us out the front door and down to the street. For the first few minutes, as the morning sun shimmers through the bare trees, neither one of us speak. It's too freaking cold! My ears sting, and I cover them with my hands.

"Here." Sam hands me a black beanie from the front pocket of his hoodie. The dog swooshes by us, oblivious to the cold.

Several minutes later, my blood warms to a degree that makes my lungs burn a little less and my breath come out thick and steamy. We fall into a comfortable pace, the dog trotting along beside us, running past sleeping brownstones, barren trees, and closed restaurants and shops. The streets are flat and sidewalks smooth, except for the scaffolding every few blocks. It's an easy, tranquil run.

Under my sweatshirt, sweat drips into my cleavage, and another trickle slides down my spine. Sam's brow is barely glistening, and his breathing is slow and steady, while I'm gulping for air.

"What happened with my sister?" I ask on a downhill stretch. Sam doesn't answer. "Was she that awful?"

"She was just being...Catie."

A chuckle releases from my lips. Big mistake. I gasp for breath. Recovering, I reply, "That's exactly how our mother used to put it."

"I've always admired you, Natalie. You do so much for Catie, and I've never heard you complain. You almost seem happy about it."

"It depends on the day."

"Today?"

"Not happy. But it's my fault."

"No, it's not."

"Is the cold freezing your brain? You were there. I pushed her into this. She was ready to give up and tell Gillian the truth, but I pressed until we found a solution."

Sam stops, and I follow suit, the dog sitting down next to me, his hot breath moist on my hand. "You didn't weave the web of lies that led Catie to this point. She spun those all on her own, and we're the schmucks who threw ourselves into her sticky threads to help her out. But the more we fight to help her, the more wrapped up we become, and soon it may do us all in."

I wipe my nose, my heart pounding in my chest. "She's my sister. I had no choice. Why did you jump in?"

"I'm a masochist."

"That's not why."

Shifting his eyes away from me, he breaks into a sprint down Hicks Street, back toward the townhouse. Pressing my toes into the concrete, I burst after him.

"What happened with Beth?"

The soggy leaves under Sam's feet kick up faster. "What does she have to do with anything?"

"I've always thought you were a typical good-looking jerk who used women. Because of what happened with you and our cousin, Beth. And because Catie always assures me that you are one. But over the last few years, I've gotten to know you pretty well, and I think I was wrong about you."

Sam stops short, his face covered in surprise. "Beth is your cousin?"

"I thought you knew that?"

"I knew you all were friends, but I didn't realize she was your cousin. It's been years since Catie's mentioned her. Until last night."

I bend down, scratching Bailey's head as he pants. "Beth got married and moved to Dallas a couple of years ago, and we only speak once in a while. But when you dated her, we were all really close. It was our shoulders she wailed on after you left her with no warning and broke her heart."

Sam shoves his hands in the front pocket of his hoodie and turns left past the large church onto Grace Court, the dog and me scampering to keep up. "I was messed up when I dated Beth. I'd just found out that Liv, my girlfriend of five years who I thought I was going to marry, was fucking some other guy. She left me, and barely two months after that, I met Beth and...well, I dumped all the shit I was feeling about Liv onto Beth. I've always regretted the way I treated her, but I was in a really crappy place. And it took a while to get out of it. It wasn't until..."

Reaching the bottom of the steps to the townhouse, I lean over my knees, sucking in air. "Until what?" I sputter.

"It doesn't matter. I told Beth I was sorry. I was awful to her, I know, but we all have fucked-up moments in our lives that we regret. Catie should realize that."

"Maybe if you told her what you just told me—"

"No. It doesn't matter anymore. I told her enough last night. I'm done with these games. I'm going to talk to Gillian."

"Wait!" Reaching out toward Sam's retreating back, I trip on a piece of uneven pavement and fall forward onto my outstretched arm.

"Ahh!" Pain explodes from my wrist to my forearm.

"Holy crap, are you okay?" Sam drops to my side. "What did you land on?"

Scooping me up, Sam carries me up the steps and inside to a bench in the foyer. I cradle my arm, wincing with every step he takes.

"I'm calling an ambulance."

"Wait!"

Sam stops.

"Don't"—I suck in sharply through the pain—"don't tell Gillian. I…dammit!" I breathe through the pain. "Just don't say anything. Please." He shakes his head as if to say I'm a fool, and I grasp his arm hard to make my point.

"Fine," he relents. "Don't move. I'm calling 911." As Sam stands up, my already-skewed equilibrium teeters over the edge, and I fall sideways onto my injured arm. A lightning bolt of pain shoots up my arm and into my head. Everything goes black.

***

When I open my eyes, I feel the soft cushions of a sofa under me. Shifting my eyes, I see the darkened fireplace in the living room to my right and several watchful faces above me. Sam is talking rapidly on the phone near the window, giving directions. Catie kneels beside me, worry etched across her face, and Karen's and Charles's curious faces float in the background.

"Look at me."

As I lift my eyes to the bright overhead lights, Max leans his face close to mine, checking my pupils.

"Don't move," Max commands. "You'll only pass out again." His face is stern and commanding, a leader on the battlefield.

89

"You're in good hands." Charles squeezes Max's shoulder, leaning over to look at me. "Max has been on the front line and dealt with worse than this."

"I have to get up." I turn to Catie, her chocolate eyes blinking up at me from the floor where she kneels beside the sofa. "What about the breakfast? And the turkey. What time is it? The turkey has to go in the oven. We have to—"

"Quiet." Max presses Catie away and takes her place, kneeling on the plush rug. "You're in shock. You need to stay still. An ambulance is on its way. Close your eyes."

"I like when you're bossy. Do it some more," I murmur.

"Quiet," he says again, but there's a smile in his voice.

Ten minutes later, an ambulance arrives. Two EMTs come inside, and Max rambles off some medical jargon regarding my condition and steps aside to let them do their work.

"I'm sorry to ruin your weekend," I say to the younger EMT, who is checking my vitals.

"We're working today whether you're injured or not. You're just making our day a little more exciting." His smile reaches his wire-rimmed glasses, and I smile back.

"Glad I could help out." Pain accosts my arm again as he kneads my wrist and forearm feeling the bones and ligaments. "Arg!"

"Sorry about that, but I don't think anything is broken. Just some torn ligaments. We won't know for sure without an X-ray though."

An X-ray would mean going to the hospital and would take half the day. I can't leave Catie alone to make the meal. It would be ruined. Everyone would be exposed.

"Can I wait until tomorrow? I really don't want to go to the hospital today."

"Don't, Natalie. It's not worth it." Sam has stepped forward, and I know he's not talking about the risk to my health.

Ignoring him, I look to the EMT with soft eyes. "I'll be real careful and come in first thing tomorrow."

"I'll put it in a sling, and you should take some Tylenol if you have it."

"Thank you." I smile, but it quickly fades as I move my wrist, and pain assaults my arm. "Do you have anything stronger? Like Percocet."

The second EMT shakes his head. "We're not allowed to give out prescription medicine."

"I have some," Max says.

"I didn't hear that," the older EMT says. "But don't take them with alcohol."

As Wire-Rimmed Glasses places my arm into a sling, the older EMT pulls out a stack of papers for me to sign since I'm declining to go to the hospital. On instinct, I reach for the pen with my right hand, but it's held tight to my body by the sling. Taking the pen into my left hand, I clumsily sign the papers. The realization of what this means suddenly hits me.

I can't cook. Not with one hand. I can't even be Catie's right-hand man, which is what we were counting on to get Catie through today. Glancing up, I know Catie has realized it too. Her face has crumbled into a look of defeat.

The jig is up.

Chapter 10
CATIE

The dawn has barely yawned into morning as the ambulance pulls away. I mumble an excuse and go up to the bedroom to begin packing. Without Natalie, it's over. There is no way I can pull this off alone. We're scheduled to shoot all the cooking today. It's faster and easier that way, according to Karen. Tomorrow we're scheduled to shoot the interview and party.

My phone buzzes. It's another text from Patrick. He's sent me about twenty since I told him what happened to Natalie's wrist.

You're a smart, clever girl. You can pull this off without Natalie. Be resourceful! And believe! If you believe it, it will come.

Has he been watching *Field of Dreams* again?

"What are you doing, Catie?"

My nerves jump under my skin at Sam's voice behind me.

"Leave me alone." I nearly hit him as I swing my suitcase off the bed. The fight from last night still hangs heavy inside me like a wet towel. No, I don't really want to hurt him, but because of his stupid confession I wrestled with sleep all night. Why would he tell me he loved me? What was the point? I've watched Sam manipulate women with his charms since I first met him, but he's never been cruel. He's never used "I love you" as a weapon. Not that I've ever witnessed.

When I first met Sam, he was just some guy dating my cousin, Beth. They went out right before I began working for *Simply Chic*. Actually, Sam's really the reason I got the job at the magazine. Beth mentioned my blog to Sam, and he passed it on to Patrick who was looking for a new writer and blogger at *Simply Chic*. By the time I got the job, Sam had dumped Beth and was already two girls past her.

Wait! That's not right. He didn't just dump Beth. He cheated on her! And when she confronted him, he dumped her. That's why I know he's a bastard.

I stride past Sam now, but my suitcase has a broken wheel making me hobble to the door. A graceful exit would have been much more satisfying.

"After all your protests and scheming, you're giving up?"

"What choice do I have? I can't fake making an entire homecoming feast on camera without Natalie."

"It's just her wrist. She can still instruct you from the sidelines."

"It won't work."

Sam blocks my path. "You don't give up. Ever."

"Don't flatter me. I didn't even want to be here in the first place." I try to shove past him, but he doesn't budge. "What do you care? You're going to reveal everything to Gillian today anyway."

"I changed my mind."

For a moment, I falter. "Why?"

His face softens. "For Natalie's sake."

Maybe I could pull this off and save my job and everyone else's along with it. No. It's better to confess now, rather than let it blow up in my face. This way, I'm the only one who will take the fall. I'll say no one else knew. And what can Gillian really do to Natalie?

Oh, God. Am I really going to do this? Am I going to walk away from everything? My whole career?

When I was broke and writing my blog on my ancient MacBook, I never dreamed I would be here: a multimedia lifestyle guru for women across America.

I let the suitcase fall on its side and collapse on top of it.

"You're right, Sam. I'm an idiot." My chin quivers, and I bite my lip to prevent an emotional outburst. I hate crying. "I've ruined everyone's lives."

"Stop feeling sorry for yourself." Despite his words, his voice has softened. Hmm, maybe he does still have feelings for me. A few near tears and he's folding like a cheap suit.

Letting my shoulders fall, I begin to sniffle loudly. In an instant, Sam's arms are around me, and my face falls into his warm chest. "I have to start filming in two hours, and I can't even scramble eggs," I say with a sob.

"I can."

"Oh, Sam!" I beam, pulling back.

Taking in my rosy cheeks and bright eyes, he recoils. "What the hell's going on?"

"What?"

"Were you really crying?"

"Of course I was." I sniffle for good measure.

"Don't." He moves away. "I can't believe I fell for that. You're a good actress, Catie. You may have missed your calling."

Crap. I may have overdone it with the theatrics. The old Sam would have laughed and helped me anyway, but this Sam looks pissed off.

"I'll still help," he says after a moment.

"Thank you, Sa—"

"I'm not doing this for you." Sam leaves, and I don't think he's coming back, but a moment later, he lays a familiar tome at my feet. "Familiarize yourself with the chapter on omelets, and then meet me downstairs. I'll help you from the sidelines, but you have to do the heavy lifting."

Sitting cross-legged in front of Julia Child's *Mastering the Art of French Cooking*, I flip to the page on omelets. Let me rephrase. I flip to the *thirteen* pages on how to make an omelet, complete with laughable pencil drawings and a description of how to fold an omelet closed with just a flick of the wrist. I've seen Natalie do it before, and it looked effortless. Could it really be that hard?

An hour later, dressed in a royal-blue Derek Lam dress and blue-suede ankle boots, my hair and makeup camera ready, I'm staring at the hot pan, the ingredients lined neatly on the counter beside me. David, the director, is hovering over my shoulder, inspecting everything on the counter and then going back to the camera to look at the shot. He gives the cameramen some instructions and then nods to Karen that he's ready.

The lights the crew set up in the kitchen, combined with the hot stove, make sweat beads form at the base of my neck. I swipe at them and then wash my hands as Mandy, the makeup artist, blots at my shimmering forehead.

"Remember, Catie," Karen says on the other side of the island, beside camera one, "it's just like in the studio, except we're not live. It takes the pressure off."

Karen steps back, and David makes a few adjustments with the cameraman he stands next to and then nods at me when the camera is rolling.

Standing in front of the ingredients, I flash my teeth and say, "Breakfast for a house full of guests can be overwhelming, and when it's for a special event like a holiday or a special party, you need something that will keep your energy high and something that tastes delicious. If you don't have much time in the morning, it's always a good idea to make something ahead." I pull out the already-cooked overnight French toast and display it for the camera. Natalie made it two days ago and brought it with us. "This overnight French toast casserole is simple and scrumptious. And there are only six ingredients that you probably already have in your cupboard." For the next few minutes, I quickly assemble the ingredients in a casserole dish—butter, a sliced French baguette, sugar, cinnamon, milk, and eggs—and slide it into the refrigerator. "Cover and refrigerate overnight, and then stick it in the oven at 350 degrees for thirty minutes in the morning. Easy peasy."

I open my mouth to give my list of five tips to make your cooking life easier on a busy morning when Gillian's sharp voice interrupts me.

"What are you wearing?"

David yells, "Cut!"

Karen presses her clipboard to her chest, taking a deep inhale. "We're in the middle of filming, Ms. Kennedy."

"Then I got here just in time. Catelyn Bloom, you should be in a traditional A-line dress with…with normal heels. And pearls."

Everyone looks down at my blue-suede ankle boots and bubble skirt.

"My wardrobe was approved by Karen and Jane, the show's stylist, a week ago."

"It wasn't approved by me." Gillian reaches toward the dress, and I step backward, worried she may try it tear it right off of me.

"We don't need your—" Karen starts.

"Leave her alone, Gillian," Charles booms. He's been sitting at the breakfast nook on his laptop during most of the filming, keeping an eye on the production but letting Karen run the show. Now he stands. "She looks great."

I jump in, glad to have Charles on my side, though I feel his support has more to do with getting under Gillian's skin than coming to my rescue. "Ms. Kennedy," I say calmly, "one of the reasons my columns and blogs are so popular is because of my youthful and fun image. The *Times* called me the 'younger, hipper Martha Stewart,' which is what this outfit reflects." It's not even that hip. Ankle boots are nothing new—plus you can't even see them behind the island—and the dress is more cute than cool.

"We need to continue filming. We're already behind." Charles sits back down, ending the conversation. Karen speaks into her head mic, and David and the cameramen, who stepped outside for a smoke, come back in, adjust the lights, and we begin the next segment.

After a quick introduction, I take a brown cage-free egg from the carton and explain the ingredients needed for the prosciutto-and-Gruyere omelet. I'm a little shaky after Gillian's interruption, and her eagle eyes are still on me as we shoot. My eyes catch Sam in my sideline, and he nods encouragingly. I bring the egg crashing down on the porcelain bowl, but the entire shell crumbles in my hand, the yolk, egg white, and half the shell sliding into the bowl.

"Shit," I mumble. David signals to do it again.

I quickly scoop up the mess, and I wipe out the bowl with a paper towel.

Try number two is slightly better, but a few pieces of shell still end up in the bowl. Since no one will be eating this omelet, I move on and crack another two eggs. Whipping the eggs, I add a dash of salt and pepper and raise the bowl to it into the pan, but Sam coughs. He's standing just out of the shot at the edge of the counter. Looking at him, he shoots his eyes to the ingredients, but I can't remember which ingredients go in before you put the eggs in the pan and which go in while it's cooking. My hand reaches into the cheese but a small shake of Sam's head stops me. There is no sound or movement from him as I sprinkle in the prosciutto and caramelized onions, explaining to the camera that you can caramelize onions ahead of time to save time in the morning. Then I pour it all into the small pan.

Sweat is beading on my forehead. A drop falls into the pan, and I cringe, but when I grab a look at David, he doesn't move. Sam eyes the bowl of Gruyere, and I sprinkle a small handful over the bubbling concoction.

"You already started." Max enters, wearing a wrinkled gray suit and old brown loafers. It's unlikely travel journalists have much use for fashion while jumping from city to city, which his outfit reflects. Even in his crumpled, worn-out suit, he still looks dashing.

"Catie!" Sam shouts.

There's smoke rising from the stove. I snatch the pan from the burner, see that the omelet is ruined, and dump it into the trash bin.

"Cut!" David yells.

"Sorry," Max says, looking at the unfortunate omelet in the trash. It was probably a blessing, since it was sure to taste as bad as it now looks.

"No, no. This is good. Let's get him in the shot." Charles lifts his head from his laptop.

"We'll need to change you into something else," Karen says, taking in Max's crumpled outfit. "Put on the gray slacks and light-blue sweater we discussed earlier."

While he's changing, a scrawny young assistant, who looks like he needs parental supervision, cleans up the mess and resets the ingredients. Back in the kitchen, Mandy tames Max's dark hair with hair wax.

"Can you do the trick where you crack an egg with one hand?" Max asks, as Mandy sweeps a powder brush across his nose.

What is he talking about? Then I remember the video blog I recently posted to correspond with my article on the best brunch places across the nation. There was a montage of close-up shots: toast popping up from a toaster, pancakes being flipped in the air, and the eggs for the omelet being cracked in one swift motion with only one hand. Natalie wanted to put a bit of flare into the segment, and I saw no harm in it. Until now.

"I don't—"

"Yes. That's a great idea," Karen says and then turns back to David, whom she's been talking to beside one of the cameras, looking at the set through the monitor.

"Really. I don't think I can. It's not—"

"Of course you can." Gillian's voice jars me. "You'll do whatever they need."

A minute later, the camera is pointed at me again. All clutter has been cleared from the counter and the ingredients reset.

Everyone eagerly watches as David yells, "Action!"

Oh, holy Hannah, please work.

The first egg is in my right hand, and I stare at it, pleading that I somehow, magically, know how to crack it using only one hand. Just a moment ago, I couldn't do it with both hands without eggshell falling into the bowl with it. Max stands beside me, and Gillian is behind camera two, watching intently. I raise my hand and crack it against the bowl, pulling back the cracked shell. The yolk and egg white drip into the bowl along with half the eggshell. Blocking the camera, I pull the eggshell out and hide it in my left hand, praying they are not going for a close-up of my hands. Max looks at me with a question mark on his face, but I ignore him. Taking the second egg, I hold it up, crack it, and—hallelujah!—no eggshell goes in the bowl. I whip the eggs and toss in prosciutto and caramelized onions to camouflage the pieces of eggshells. Then I pour it all into the pan, wait for it to solidify, and fold it over. It looks perfect.

Scooping it onto a plate, I place it on the counter and wait for David to get the shot of the finished dish. Then I hand it to Sam, who is off camera, and give him a tiny shake of my head and mouth *don't eat.*

"Show me how to crack an egg like that," Max says next to me.

"It's too tricky."

"Do it." Gillian is pushing the cameraman next to her closer to me. He looks ready to punch her. David's face reflects the cameraman's annoyance, and he looks to Karen, who tells them to get the shot.

Smiling widely at the camera, then at Max, I place the egg in his hand. "The best way to learn is to do it yourself." Before anyone can argue, I continue. "Hit it against the bowl with enough force to crack it, then ease the egg apart with your fingers, separating the shell." I step aside. Max grips the egg and, for a moment, looks at me, his mouth opening to say something; then he looks, shrugs, and smashes the egg onto the side of the bowl, yellow goo and broken shell falling onto the counter in a messy glop.

"He can break a story, but he can't break an egg," I quip to the camera, and David yells cut.

One thing I've learned working on *Wake Up, America!* is, when all else fails, a good one-liner saves everything.

***

Riding on my high from the earlier success in front of the camera, I rush out of the kitchen and pull up all of Natalie's notes for the homecoming meal I'm preparing in less than an hour. Natalie has been passed out in her room since this morning, and I fear she won't be able to help, even from the sidelines.

The breakfast shoot was barely a success, but I'm feeling confident I can pull this off with a little Catelyn Bloom flare. Natalie said she was up half the night cooking and prepping.

The hard part is done. The rest should be dumping it all together and putting it in the oven.

But when I enter the kitchen to set up my workspace for filming, the sound of metal crashing to the floor jars me. Natalie stands in front of the counter; the silverware drawer and all its contents are spilled at her feet.

"Oopsy."

Sitting cross-legged on the floor, Natalie haphazardly scoops the silverware up with her left hand and tries to organize it back into the drawer, missing every time. Her tongue pressing against her bottom lip, she tries again.

When that fails, she begins to giggle.

"What's wrong with you?" I ask, my heart picking up pace. Her eyes are hazy and don't quite meet mine. "How many painkillers did you take?"

"Two. No, three. No, two. No...I don't remember."

I've already come to terms with the fact that Natalie can't physically help me in the kitchen today, but the one thing I was counting on is her mind, which is now zoned out on painkillers.

"Oh!" Natalie yelps, as she misses the stool she was climbing on and crashes to the floor. She begins laughing uncontrollably.

"Natalie," I say. "Natalie!"

But she's lost it.

Just then, my phone pings twice. The first is a text from Patrick asking how everything is going. I ignore it. The second is a reminder that my first mortgage payment is due. In all the madness, I almost forgot I had real responsibilities in the real world. Natalie can't fall apart now. I know she's eager to leave her job and finally start her own restaurant and gourmet shop. For one satisfying moment, sinking down to the floor to meet Natalie in her hysteria, I almost slip under with her. The current of desperation is strong inside me, and part of me wants it to take me under and for this to be over.

But Patrick's and Sam's faces float behind my eyes, and I know I can't do it. When Natalie recovers, she'll blame herself for any repercussions, even though it's my fault we're all in this ridiculous mess.

Natalie's manic laughter dies down, and she rests her head on my shoulder, breathing deeply.

"Nat? I know you're hurt, but I need you."

"I know, Little Bee."

Hearing my pet name from childhood makes my chin quiver, and I press my lips together tightly to stop any emotions from rising past my throat.

"Do you think you can discreetly guide me along on this crazy merry-go-round that's about to start?"

Natalie lifts her head, swipes the smudges of mascara from under her eyes, and gives me a lopsided grin. "Chin up! This is going to be fun!"

The wave that was taking me under releases its grip slightly. It might all work out after all. Still, I wish I had her enthusiasm.

Or one of her Percocets.

Chapter 11

CATIE

"The oven isn't on!"

I almost drop the newly-whipped-together cheesecakes I'm holding. "What?"

"The oven isn't on!" Natalie says in an exaggerated stage whisper.

Filming has momentarily stopped while Charles and Karen step aside to discuss the schedule, since the filming of me cooking the meal has turned into an all-afternoon affair. The dinner shoot may have to be delayed. David and the small crew have gone outside to take a cigarette and phone break.

Sam and Max sit at the breakfast nook, Sam with an amused look on his face and Max bemused at the chaos around him.

"Turn it on," I urge, my hands occupied by the cakes.

Natalie teeters off the stool, which she has fallen off of twice already, and punches several buttons on the oven.

"Now open it."

As the oven door falls down, everything turns to slow motion as I gape inside the oven at the very big, very raw turkey staring back.

"The turkey!"

Natalie claps her hands as if I've just presented her with a new car or designer knife set. She's been like this all afternoon. It would have been better if she'd left the kitchen entirely, but she refused, and when I tried to push her out, she started making such a scene that I let her stay. The kitchen has been filled all day with the crew, cameras, and Max all watching us with sharp eyes.

My eyes flick to Sam for help, but he just continues to smile his Cheshire cat grin that he's had all day. Despite his assertions, he has been of no assistance. It's as if he wants me to fail. Maybe that's his new game. Instead of telling Gillian the truth, he's letting me dig my own grave. He is a cruel, cruel man.

Sliding the pan of cakes onto the top rack of the oven, I whisper to Natalie, "How long does it take a turkey to cook?"

"Four hours."

"Four hours!" I scream and then lower my voice. "We're meant to be filming this damn meal in the dining room in an hour."

Max's voice interrupts us from across the room. "Is there a problem? Can I help?"

"No!" we both yell.

"Can't we just turn the oven up really high?" I ask, keeping my voice down. Natalie bends over in a fit of laughter in lieu of an answer. I'm glad someone thinks this is hysterical, because I'm about to Sylvia Plath myself right in that oven.

The kitchen door swings open, and Charles and Gillian walk in with grim looks on their faces. "The kitchen is wrapped. Bring the meal into the dining room. We'll shoot it now." Charles takes in my appearance. "Mandy!"

"Do you have another dress?" Mandy asks when she sees me.

"Yes."

"Good. Change, fix your hair, and then I'll touch up your makeup."

"We're way over schedule, so the dinner is going to be the last shot of the day. The dinner shoot shouldn't take long since there's no audio. We only need shots of the food on display and Max, Catelyn, Sam, Gillian, and the dog sitting around the table eating." Charles hands me a new shot list and schedule. "We moved the cocktail shoot to tomorrow. We'll film it before we leave for the party at the hotel."

"Aren't you going to be in the dinner shoot?" I ask. He is Gillian's husband, and he's been absent from everything we've filmed so far.

"No. I leave the limelight to my wife. She looks much better in it," he says and leaves, Gillian rolling her eyes at his back as she follows him out.

Hallelujah! They're done shooting the kitchen! But what am I going to do about the meal? There's nothing edible or pretty in sight. The turkey is raw! The cakes aren't cooked. The gravy is burned. And the soup was ruined when Natalie handed me sugar instead of salt. The only edible food is the bread rolls.

Maybe we don't need an edible meal. They only need a brief shot of us all around the table. We don't have to actually be eating the food. The dinner is going to be cut up and inserted into part of a montage. According to Karen, the whole special is a ten-minute segment, mainly featuring me cooking, shots of Max playing with the dog and relaxing, me interviewing him, and then ending with the party. We can easily film and cut in a shot of the prepared feast later. Once I actually, you know, cook the turkey. And the rest of the meal!

But how would I explain it to Gillian? She'd want to know what the hell happened to the meal I've been preparing and shooting in the kitchen and why every part of it is inedible. Snoring from the bench of the breakfast nook draws my attention, momentarily. It's Natalie.

"I think the energizer bunny has finally run out of batteries," Sam quips.

"Can you take her upstairs?" I ask.

Max scoops her up before Sam can respond. "I'll take her." The dog bounds after him, knocking into me. My hand reaches out for the counter and knocks the entire breadbasket onto the floor.

"Dammit! That was the only palatable thing left in this kitchen," I yell to the only person there, Sam. "And you were completely useless today."

"Don't you dare put this on me. You're the one screwing this up." Sam kicks the basket, and it flies across the kitchen.

"I'm sorry...I didn't mean...I wasn't blaming...I've got a lot going on!"

After the outburst, all the wind goes out of my sails. All that matters is I have no meal to serve for a dinner that's meant to be on the table right now. My face is smeared with gravy, my dress is covered in cake batter, and my hair has gone limp from the heat of the lights and stress. I don't know how much longer I can continue this.

There are a half-dozen serving platters laid out but no food to put on them.

Kicking off my shoes, I pull over a half-empty bottle of Malbec. Hell, why not? It's almost a relief to know it's over. I just need a little liquid courage before I go in there and face Gillian.

A knock on the front door draws Sam away. There's rustling as a woman in a white smock follows Sam into the kitchen and places two large boxes filled with various sizes of brown bags and foil containers on the kitchen table. She hands Sam a piece of paper, he signs it, and the woman exits.

"Grab the serving platters and start unpacking the food."

Peering into one of the boxes, I see a steaming hot, fully cooked turkey. And there's more. Each container I open or bag I unpack brings another surprise: mashed potatoes, green beans, rolls, bacon-and-leek soup, and two perfect cheesecakes.

I yelp. I scream. My limp insides have sprung to life as adrenaline fills my body, and I jump up and down. I'm so ecstatic I forget to be mad or annoyed or whatever at Sam, and I jump on him, hugging him and laughing. "Thank you, thank you, thank you!"

His arms tighten around me. All the worry and fear I've been wrapped up in fades away, and my heart swells in my chest for everything Sam has done for me.

"Thank you," I whisper into his ear.

"You're welcome." He pulls me back and looks at me with such intensity my chest tightens to the point it hurts.

"Quick. Let's get this stuff into the serving dishes before anyone sees." Escaping Sam's embrace, I keep my head buried in the boxes and bags. My chest aches from the emotions wrestling inside me. Yes, I liked Sam when I first met him. I liked him a lot, but I pushed those feelings aside. It wasn't hard. I'd gotten good at controlling my feelings for the opposite sex by then. And when he showed his true colors and destroyed Beth's heart, I made sure any signs of those feelings were wrangled and locked in a cage deep inside me. If the lock were to break open, I don't think I could handle the wild emotions that would run free and pummel my heart and soul.

If Sam ever knew the truth, I'd lose all control. And that scares the hell out of me. More than this weekend. More than losing my job. More than anything in my life.

Chapter 12

NATALIE

The last twenty-four hours are a whirlwind of blurry images that I can't grasp. The room where I lie now is dark, but the streaks of light peaking through the curtains above the bed tell me it's daytime. A groan escapes my lips as I sit up, my head and wrist throbbing.

"Move slowly."

I yelp at the deep voice in the darkness. "Who's there?"

The light from the table lamp flicks on, illuminating Max lying on the floor of my tiny room, Bailey sleeping next to him.

"Where is everybody?"

"Prepping for the interview and party."

"I thought the interview was tomorrow."

"This is tomorrow." Max smiles apologetically, as if it's his fault I slept half a day.

I hold my head, trying to recall memories I can't quite grasp. "What happened?"

"You drank and took very strong painkillers."

"Oopsy." I bite my lip, feeling uncomfortable under his intense gaze.

"I warned you to be careful when I gave you those pills." There's a short pause and then a small smile plays on Max's lips. "You were acting a little crazy, talking about you being Cyrano de Bergerac, and Catie was the other guy who looked good but had no talent."

My face flushes from worry and the mound of blankets on me, and I slide them off. I stretch the kinks out of my arms, being careful of my wrist. "What else did I say?"

"Oh, um…you…you're wearing…" Max falters, averting his eyes. Looking down, I yank the sheet over my chest; my body is clad in a white lace bra and underwear. At least I wore a matching pair yesterday.

Keeping his head turned, Max takes the folded jeans and blue blouse from the floor next to him and hands them to me. "You took them off. Or tried to." I'm struggling to get my injured arm through the cap sleeves, and Max gently slides the top over my head and chest, keeping his face turned away. "I helped a little. Because of your wrist," he adds, the heat from his body close to mine as he pulls the blouse down my torso. I look into his eyes, only inches from me, and I'm surprised to see pain in them. I want to know why, but he stands, breaking the connection.

"How was the meal? Did Catie, er…was everything okay?" I slide the curtains open above the bed, letting light pour into the room. Bailey stirs and stretches his front paws on the floor, opening his mouth in a big yawn.

"In the end, the meal came together and the food was amazing." Max sits, rubbing Bailey between his ears. "Which was surprising."

"What do you mean? Why?"

"There were a few…incidents."

"Sometimes Catie gets nervous in front of the camera. She's never filmed anything like this." Which isn't really true. When a camera is on her, Catie is quick on her toes and exudes confidence and calm. Even if she's freaking out on the inside, she keeps it together on the outside.

Amusement crosses Max's face. "I guess that explains why she was almost manic during filming. You both were, but whenever anything went wrong, which was a lot of things, Catie always had a witty comeback or clever save. And you were right there beside her. Not on camera, but yelling at her from the sidelines. I think you thought you were being discreet."

That doesn't sound like Catie's usual calm-and-collected self. Maybe the pressure is starting to get to her.

"Did Catie seem happy with it?"

"Oh, she was very happy in the end." The glimmer in Max's eyes as he talks about Catie makes my already-queasy stomach turn even more. "She's a pro."

"How was the dinner shoot?"

Bailey suddenly leaps onto the bed and begins licking my face. I dodge his soft, wet tongue, but it's hard with one able arm.

"Bailey, sit," Max commands.

Immediately, the dog sits on his hind legs next to me. I pet the soft fur on the dog's back, and it nuzzles in next to me.

"Wow. You have a way with this one," I say.

"Dogs like to know who's in control. It's in their nature." Max leans over and scratches behind Bailey's ear.

Max wears a crumpled suit without the jacket, which I notice is bunched up on the floor like a makeshift pillow. "Did you sleep here?"

Picking up the jacket, he smooths his hands over it, but it stays a wrinkled mess. "Mixing Percocet and alcohol is dangerous."

My heart flutters. "You were worried?"

"I've seen firsthand how lethal the combination can be." Max stands, and then Bailey leaps off the bed and waits by the door. "Be careful. Use one or the other to numb what's bothering you, because I know it's more than your arm."

He exits, and there's a rustling outside the door and low voices, then the lilt of female laughter. As the sound of footsteps fade, the door opens.

"Good morning!" Catie sings.

The sun reflecting off her red-sequined gown sends a disco ball of lights around the room. Her hair has been swept up in a messy bun, and her eyes pop from her smoky eye makeup.

"Up, up," she trills. "You're needed downstairs, and then you have to get dressed for the party."

"I thought my official duties were done." All the filming in the kitchen and dining room where scheduled for yesterday.

"They want to shoot me making Max's favorite whiskey cocktail." Catie sits on the bed. "I was hoping you could help set it up. It's going to be a quick shot of me mixing the drinks before the party."

"All right." I stand, blood rushing down my body, making my head spin and my arm ache. "Pass me those pills."

Catie takes them and holds them behind her back. "Yesterday was a near disaster with you on these pills. It would have exploded in our faces if Sam hadn't had a back-up plan."

"What happened?"

"Sam preordered a whole catered meal nearly identical to what I prepared, except it was all cooked and edible."

"What about the filming?" I sit back against the headboard, my stomach growling from hunger. "Max made it sound like a near disaster."

"It was a mess, but there's enough footage they can cut together and make it work. Karen and David were a bit annoyed, but luckily the dinner went smoothly. There was no sound recorded since it's being cut into a montage, so we just had several cameras pointed at us and ate and laughed and talked until they had enough footage."

"What about Sam?" I smooth my hair and wipe the mascara smudges from under my eyes. Suddenly, I'm ravenous.

"He kept his back to the camera. They mainly focused on Max, Gillian, me, and the dog. It was all happy, happy, happy." Catie moves toward me. "You look weak. Do you want me to bring you up a plate of the overnight French toast?"

"Yes." I feel energized just at the thought of the food. "Is it edible?"

"It's delicious. Gillian almost ate the entire dish." Catie laughs. "Feel free to use the big tub in the master suite if you want. We need to be ready to go by noon, and it's already past nine."

"Ready for what?"

"The party."

My arm throbs in protest. "I'm staying here."

"I wouldn't care, but when I bumped into Max in the hall he insisted you come. He's worried you're gonna overdose or something and doesn't want you to be left alone here." Catie scrapes her fingers through the back of her hair, tucking in a couple loose strands. "Isn't he thoughtful."

"I don't have anything to wear," I say, glad to have an excuse to stay behind.

"You can borrow one of the extra gowns I brought. You'll look great in the black lace Nicole Miller. And it's strapless, so you won't have to shove your arm through a sleeve." Sweeping out of the room, Catie doesn't wait for an answer.

***

As I wait in the kitchen for Catie to finish the cocktail segment in the living room, I swallow another painkiller. The one I took this morning has worn off, and my arm is aching again. Max walks in from the living room with Bailey by his side and a whiskey cocktail in his hand.

"Did you want one?" Max asks, indicating the cocktail.

In response, my head pounds, remembering the wine-and-painkiller cocktail I mixed together last night.

"No, thanks."

"Where did your sister go to culinary school?" Max asks, sitting on the bench in the breakfast nook.

This isn't the time or place I want to be dodging questions about my sister, so I ignore him, opening the refrigerator and pulling out a bag of grapes.

"I couldn't find any info in her bio on the *Simply Chic* website. In fact, I couldn't find one recipe on her blog the first year it was online."

I'm spared answering as the dog bounds across the kitchen, knocks over the water bowl, and jumps toward me with his paws out.

"No!" I yelp, scooting backward, dropping the grapes I'm holding onto the ground. Normally, I wouldn't care if a dog jumped up on me, but the dress I'm wearing has a fine lace overlay that would be ruined if one of the claws got into it. Catie would kill me. She borrowed it from the beauty editor at *Simply Chic*. Pulling the long gown above my knees, I back up and jump onto the bench where Max sits, the dog bounding toward me again.

Before I can figure out an exit strategy, the dog jumps onto the bench. "Down, boy! Sit!" Taking my pointed Choo off, I swing it toward the dog but miss, nailing Max in the groin.

"Ah!" he yelps, hunching over in pain as the dog halts, coming to Max's side.

"Oh my God! I'm so sorry." I kneel next to him. "Is it, um, broken?"

Unable to speak, Max shakes his head.

"Do you need ice?" I'm already across the kitchen, my left hand in the freezer, clumsily grasping several chunks of ice.

Max's hands are holding his thighs, and he's breathing deeply, but a chuckle escapes his lips when he sees the ice dripping from my fingers.

"No, no. No ice," he says, scooting back.

Undeterred, I press the ice to his pants.

"Get off!"

There's a clatter as the cubes spills all over the floor. I'm surprised by his outburst. "Sorry. I was trying to help."

"I know." Max takes a deep breath, his face still scrunched in pain. "Just give me a little space."

Both Bailey and I back away, I dump the rest of the melting ice into the kitchen sink, and the dog begins to devour the spilled grapes.

"No!"

I jump at Max's voice.

"The dog! Stop him!"

"What?! What do you mean?"

"Grapes could kill him!"

Grabbing the dog's collar, I pull Bailey away from the few grapes left on the floor and place him next to Max.

"What is all the noise?" Gillian's voice booms into the room. "We're filming in there."

"The dog, ma'am," I explain. "He ate some grapes."

Gillian crosses her arms, unimpressed.

"Grapes can be lethal for dogs, Aunt Gilli," Max explains.

My breath catches. I never knew that.

Gillian pulls her phone out, a long red nail hovering over the screen. "Do I need to call 911?"

"No," Max says, inspecting the dog. "We just need to keep a close eye on him."

Catie stands in the kitchen doorway, a cocktail shaker in her hand. "Is everyone okay?"

"Fine." Gillian whisks past her, heading back into the living room.

I explain what happened as Max inspects Bailey's eyes and mouth.

"Are you both okay?"

"It's unlikely Bailey will have a reaction, but I'll keep him close the rest of the day, just to make sure." Max rubs Bailey's head, and the dog's tail wags enthusiastically.

I take Catie's arm, and we leave Max to attend to the dog. In the living room, the sound of Sam's voice in the foyer makes Catie halt. She pulls me near the door to the foyer, out of sight, and listens. Across the room, David and one cameraman pack up two large duffel bags and leave the room, filming apparently complete. Catie puts the sweating shaker down on the bookshelf next to her.

"I've been reading the back copies of *Edge* magazine, young man," Gillian is saying. "It's not my taste, but it does well amongst our young male readers. You're a very good writer and find the most intriguing characters for your human-interest stories."

"Thank you, ma'am." His words are casual, but there's an eagerness in his voice.

"Your stories are very relatable, and I think they would appeal to a wider audience if given the chance."

"What are we doing?" I whisper. My feet already hurt from my four-inch stilettos. I'm not used to wearing heels. Waving her hand, Catie indicates for me to be quiet.

"What was it you needed to talk to me about?" Gillian asks.

"Oh, well, the filming."

"Yes, isn't it wonderful? We'll be getting so much exposure for your wife and the magazine. And it wouldn't do you any harm to get your face out there."

"That's not an option." Sam's voice is firm.

The glass in Catie's hand is being strangled. I don't know what's going on between those two, but they have been tense around each other all morning. They're covering it up, and no one else would notice, but I can spot their caustic remarks and prickly attitudes a mile away.

"What if he says something?" Catie scoots closer toward the foyer doors.

"Why would he do that?" Grabbing the edge of the bookcase, I still my swaying body. The painkillers are swimming into my bloodstream.

"He hates me."

"Why?"

"He told me he loves me."

"What?!" In less than two seconds, I pull Catie across the room. "Spill."

Words tumbling out, Catie explains everything that happened on the first night and Sam's confession and subsequent take back.

"Do you love him?"

"No! Absolutely not. And he doesn't love me. He's just confused. It's a rare occasion a girl turns him down." The wood floor is growing shiny where Catie's right shoe is rubbing it fiercely. "You always want the one you can't have and all that."

"Then why are you so worried?"

The little veins in Catie's neck pop out. "Because he could ruin everything. He could be out there right now telling Gillian the truth. When it comes to his work, Sam is very ethical."

Not waiting for my response, Catie hurries to the other side of the room and resumes her position, tucked behind the

116

doorway to the foyer, listening to Sam and Gillian, who are still in conversation. Against my better judgment, I follow, if only to save Catie from herself.

"I'm very impressed by you and everything you've done for the adventure features in the magazine and online content." Through a crack in the door, I see Gillian place her hand on Sam's shoulder, and Sam beams from the attention. "Next fall, we're starting a new sports e-zine, focused only on extreme sports."

"That sounds like a great idea. Who is—"

"I need an honest and reliable editor," Gillian continues. "I can see the PR campaign now, Samuel Harding, Catelyn Bloom's husband, launches an exciting new magazine…"

"That will be the campaign?" Sam is standing at full attention. "And you want me to run the entire magazine?"

"Absolutely. You're just the kind of couple the public will eat up, so to speak. And what a great way to introduce you. On national television. I couldn't have planned it more perfectly."

"Right. Right." Sam is rubbing his forehead, looking weary and shell shocked.

"Think about it, and let me know."

I turn to Catie. "I thought Sam didn't want to be on TV?"

"Are those damn vans loaded yet?" We press against the wall as Gillian walks toward the kitchen. After a full minute, Sam walks into the living room and sits alone on one of the armchairs in front of the fireplace, looking like a lost man.

"You look dashing," I say, approaching.

His eyes stay focused on the blue-and-white rug his feet rest on. "She offered me a magazine. But—"

"That's great!" The enthusiasm in Catie's voice sounds forced.

"It's not great!" he blasts. "She made it clear it wouldn't be possible if we weren't married."

"I'm sorry, Sam," I pipe in. "If I hadn't pushed Catie and you to do this, we wouldn't be in this mess."

"It's not your fault, Natalie," Catie snaps. "And it's not mine, either. We're all adults. We each made the decision to be here. Don't act like a victim, Sam."

I'm surprised that Catie is being so insensitive. It's as if she wants to push Sam away.

"I thought it would just be a little white lie. It seemed like an adventure when we all agreed to it," I say, trying to soften Catie's words.

"This adventure," Sam says, turning fierce eyes on Catie, "just turned into a shitstorm. Once the truth comes out—and it will, it always does—Gillian will never give me the promotion. Hell, I'll be lucky to keep my job."

He stands abruptly.

Karen walks into the room. "The van is packed, and the cars are ready to go to the hotel."

Sam follows Karen, and Catie catches up to him and slides her hand into his. There's a slight hesitation before Sam tightens his grip.

"Just what I'm in the mood for," Sam deadpans. "A party."

Chapter 13
CATIE

"What made you become a travel writer?"

I'm reading from the script Karen handed me before the filming began. It takes all my strength not to roll my eyes at half the questions, which are mostly glib and superficial. This is the first one to pique my interest, and I lean in.

Max smiles, the dog snuggled up next to him on the small gray sofa we sit on, our knees almost touching. It's meant to be an intimate, cozy interview, but I feel slightly awkward dressed up in my red gown, Max in his tuxedo. Karen and Gillian are eating it up. I guess glamour and tragic heroes sell.

"Growing up, I dreamed of being the next Kerouac or Burroughs. In college, my friends and I would spend late nights drinking whiskey and getting high and writing what we thought was poignant prose and edgy poetry. I remember writing a dark piece I called "Annihilation," and after I read it to my creative-writing class, I ate the paper it was written on. My teacher was not impressed. Neither were most of the students."

I laugh. Max has the type of self-deprecating humor that endears me to him and will charm the viewers. I never noticed it before, and maybe he hasn't shown it to me. In reality, I probably haven't given Max or his life before this weekend much thought. I've been so focused on getting through the filming that I forgot what the special is really about. This man.

I scan the next card and ask, "Is that when you moved to India—after college?"

"I tried for years to make a living as a freelance writer with no luck and no money. Even though my aunt owns a media conglomerate, I didn't use her to get a leg up in my writing career. Not at first." Max shifts, and the dog lifts its head, licking Max's cheek. "I moved to Mumbai to teach English. I was bored and wanted to travel but had no money. Teaching gave me enough income to live in a nice apartment with a little extra money each month to travel. What it also gave me was my first writing gig. The newspaper associated with the school where I taught classes wanted an expat's view of living in Mumbai. That led to other writing gigs and, most importantly, connections to editors. I traveled and taught all over Asia for five years, all the while building my portfolio. And soon I realized I was sick of freelancing, of not knowing when the next job would come. I wanted something more secure."

"That's when you contacted your aunt?" I glance off-camera to where Gillian sits in her black gown on the edge of one of the director chairs, her hair scraped back into a tight ponytail, making her eyes slant at the edges.

"No. I wasn't sure what my next step was going to be." Max sits back and places his ankle on his opposite knee. "That's when my aunt called out of the blue and offered me the position."

"He made me beg," Gillian hollers.

"Only a little." Max smiles sheepishly. "I wasn't sure I was ready to work for the man. Plus—"

"Woman!" Gillian shouts, but there's a smile in her voice.

"Right, woman."

The crew laughs, and Mandy takes this chance to smooth my hair and powder Max's forehead. Gillian decided not to be part of the interview at the last minute. She felt it would benefit the viewers more to focus on Max and me. In other words, she thought it would benefit her bottom line more to only have Catelyn Bloom and Max Euston in front of the camera.

"Please, continue," Karen says from the tall director's chair she sits in next to David.

"A day after Gillian e-mailed me with the offer, the editor at one of her competitors called and offered me a position." Max looks off camera and smiles at Gillian. "I jokingly sent Gillian an e-mail with the offer from the competitor and said she better act quick and sweeten the deal."

"And did she?"

"Of course, but I didn't take it. I mean, I took the position but not the extra money or benefits she offered to counter the competitor." Max looks directly at Gillian. "I would have worked for you for half the pay."

"Done!" Gillian yells.

Karen whispers something to David, and he yells, "Cut!" I take a sip of water and glance out into the space beyond us. We've set up the interview in the small library at the edge of the lobby of The Parker Inn, one of the oldest hotels in Downtown Brooklyn. The muffled sounds of the party on the other side of the door can be heard, and I wish we were done with this interview and enjoying the party. The hotel manager said it is busier than usual as word spread about the filming in the hotel.

"Let's move on to Greece," Karen says.

The lights and cameras are adjusted, and when everything is set, we begin again.

Reading the notes, I ask, "What happened that day in Greece?"

"As most major events in life, it started out like any other day. I was on my way to interview this adventure junky who was about to BASE jump off the seaside cliffs in Santorini. I was on a moped when I saw this white van jump a curb onto a sidewalk and cut off this mother and daughter. Three men jumped out, one of them grabbed the girl, and the other two held off the mother, who was screaming. Then they sped off with the girl. I didn't even think. I just took off after them. About five miles ahead, they stopped in an empty church parking lot."

"Did they know you were following them?"

"At that point, I assumed they didn't because they hadn't been swerving or driving at high speeds or anything to lose me. But when I slowed down next to the driveway, the two bigger men jumped out of the back of the van and zeroed in on me, ready for a fight. One held up his fists, which were massive, and the other one had a metal pipe in his hand." He takes a deep breath, smoothing his wavy hair off his forehead, and looks at the camera. "But what they didn't see was the small knife in my hand. When I saw them coming at me, I'd pulled it off my belt and had it ready just in case."

"And you stabbed both men before they could touch to you," I continue for him.

"Yes." Max sits on the edge of the sofa, his eyes bright with the adrenaline from the memory. "I ducked when one of them swung the pipe at my head, and with two swift movements, I cut the first one's ankle and stabbed the other one's knee, which is when I lost the knife. At that point, the driver realized the two men were down and jerked the van forward, causing the little girl, who was still in the back of the van, to roll out as he sped off. I picked her up and called the police, and as I was explaining what happened, everything went black."

"One of the men had recovered and hit Max in the back of the head with the pipe," I turn to the camera and explain. "When the police arrived, they found Max unconscious and the injured men were a half mile down the road, carrying the girl. They didn't get far with their injuries."

"Luckily." Max's gaze shifts off-camera, his eyes focused on one of the floor-to-ceiling bookcases that line the walls, looking lost in his memories.

"And the girl was rescued, uninjured, and returned to her mother. It had been the girl's father, a criminal on the run, who had tried to kidnap her," I continue to the camera, my fingers reaching for Max's hand, bringing him back. He blinks rapidly and refocuses on me. "If Max hadn't intervened, the father would have sold her into child trafficking." I pull my hand back and read my notes. "Max saved her from a dark and horrible life that surely would have killed her."

I hold back a cringe as I finish the segment. *Who writes this crap?*

We take a break, and I send a quick update to Patrick as the crew readjusts the camera, lights, and microphones for the next segment. I've never done a taped interview but find it much more relaxing than the cooking segments. Everything is scripted, and all I have to do is sit and parrot what's written on the interview cards.

It sounds like you pulled it off! Patrick texts.

Don't jinx it! I respond.

He sends me back several thumbs-ups and smiley faces.

I'm not ready to match his enthusiasm. The night's not over.

When the filming begins again, I turn back to Max, compose myself, and read over the next set of questions.

"What went through your mind when you woke up in the hospital and had no memory?"

"Not much."

I laugh, happy that Max has a sense of humor. A rosy hue has returned to his chiseled cheeks now that we've moved on from his chase and rescue. It only happened a few months ago, and the events must still be raw in his mind.

"It was strange. Like searching for a word at the tip of your tongue, except it's your whole life you can't remember." Max looks at his clasped hands. "I couldn't even remember my fi...er...any of my friends' names or faces," Max continues. "A couple other travel reporters and friends came to visit me in the hospital in Greece, but nothing triggered any memories. Even seeing the little girl I saved didn't trigger my memories. Then one day, Jess was talking about Trixie, my childhood dog, and it all came flooding back."

"Who's Jess?"

Max looks startled. "Oh. Um, a soldier from a unit I reported on in Afghanistan for a couple of months. Jessica Crossman."

There's more to that story, but this isn't meant to be an investigative piece. Still I pry a little deeper.

"Were you close?"

Max stiffens. "You latch onto anything familiar when traveling. It's a product of the nomad life. Our stories crossed paths often."

Voices and music blast into the room as the double doors open and two guests tumble in, laughing and kissing. When they see us, they quickly straighten, apologize, and rush out in a fit of giggles.

David yells, "Cut!" And there's movement around the room as the crew relaxes, taking gulps from their venti coffee cups, and I suspect something stronger in David's glass tumbler. I don't blame him; it's been a long couple of days for the crew. When the lights hit us again, I dab at a droplet of sweat running down my brow. Mandy powders me again and reapplies my crimson lipstick and swipes a quick brush of powder over Max's forehead and nose before he can protest.

"Let's talk more about the dog and regaining your memory," Karen says and signals to David to continue shooting.

"Why do you think your childhood dog, Trixie, triggered your memories? What was so special about her?" I begin, crossing my red stilettos at my ankles.

"She wasn't your typical dog that played a lot of fetch, like a golden retriever or lab, but she loved to run around, and we played outside for hours until she collapsed in my bed at the end of the day. After my parents died when I was fifteen, Trixie was the only immediate family I had left. I'm not surprised she's what brought back my memories. Most of my days with her were the happiest of my life." Max scratches the dog next to him behind his ears, and Bailey pops his head up, looking adoringly at Max. "It's been nice having another greyhound around. I mean, having her around."

"Wait. Stop. Cut." Gillian is on her feet, pacing like a panther. "You haven't mentioned anything about what happened to you when you were reporting in Afghanistan. About what you'd already been through when you found yourself in another terrifying situation in Greece. The viewers need to know all the reasons why Max is a hero. It's the hook of the whole special."

"We covered some of it in the interview, and they'll be more in voice-overs and montage when we edit," Karen says, looking exhausted, either by the filming or Gillian, or maybe both.

"No. I want the war story to be filmed with Catelyn Bloom. Now." Gillian stops moving and stares at Karen.

After a quick glance at her watch, Karen signals David to get the shot ready. There are a few groans from the crew, but a minute later, we're all back in position. I don't have any notes on what Gillian is talking about, so I have to wing it.

"This wasn't your first brush with near tragedy." I face Max, the two cameras pointed at us. "What happened to you in Afghanistan?"

Max considers his answer. "As much as I enjoy travel writing, I longed for something deeper. When I was still in India, I met a couple of soldiers who were on leave, and I decided to go back with them and interview their unit about the ongoing war efforts. A two-day gig turned into two months, and I followed their unit around and reported on their experiences. It had been a relatively quiet couple of months; most of the action had been over for more than a year by then."

"But something happened," I prompt, involuntarily moving closer, eager for the story.

"It was meant to be my last day, and it was chaotic organizing everything before I left. We were running late because of trouble with one of the trucks. A spark plug, I think. It was the middle of July and close to a hundred degrees, and we needed a place to keep cool, so we stepped into a small café. The next thing I remember is someone screaming, and I turned and saw a man wearing a bomb strapped to his chest. Something must have gone wrong because he mumbled some words—a prayer—and braced himself, but nothing happened. Then two men followed behind him with PK machine guns."

My mouth is agape, and I shut it. It's not very professional to look like I don't know what's coming, but I'm enthralled. "What was going through your mind?"

"Nothing and everything. You don't have time to think, only react. I'm not a soldier, but after two months following a unit, I'd learned to move like one. Parks and Corban, two of the soldiers form the unit, charged the suicide bomber and took him down, but he had a knife and sliced them both

126

several times before they got him. Crossman, Meeks, and I went for the two gunmen. We took them down quickly, but they fired several rounds before we got to them. I took one in my shoulder, Meeks took one in the chest, and Crossman...Crossman, um, she took one in the right bicep."

"And everyone was okay?"

Max drops his head. "No. We...they lost Meeks."

My life suddenly seems ridiculous in comparison. Max risked his life to reveal the truths of war. I reveal what's in my special chicken potpie that will make your husband turn off that Monday-night game and come to the dinner table.

"Witnessing so many violent deaths at once disrupts your entire universe." Max barrels on, his mind focused on the memories. "After that, I couldn't go back. War journalism wasn't for me. I have great respect for the journalists who can throw themselves into that world. But when they're thrust back into everyday life, they can't relate. Sometimes they can barely function. I didn't want that. I'd already been through enough tragedy in my life to not go looking for more."

I press my lips together, my heart aching for him. The pain in his eyes is raw. He's done a good job this weekend keeping his emotions in check and behaving like a normal guy, but he's got real demons inside him. It must take all his strength to mimic a normal life. No wonder he clings to the dog—even if it's a fraud—as if he's Max's lifeline.

"Do you resent being here?" The words are out before I realize it. There's rustling behind the camera.

Blinking several times, Max looks at me, taking in his surroundings. "No. Not at all. You need to get back to the quote-unqoute *real world*. I can't live the rest of my life in the past."

"Cut!" Karen steps forward from behind the camera. "Let's take five." She pulls a plastic, folding chair up in front of Max and me. "You're doing great. We don't need much more. Let's wrap up with Max's plans for the future. David."

Mindy steps in and touches up my makeup and adjusts my red-sequined dress, avoiding the mic discreetly pinned to the tight bodice. When David says, "Action," I turn back to Max.

"You lost your parents, witnessed a grave tragedy in Afghanistan, saved a girl from kidnapping, and woke up without any memories to discover you're a national hero and media sensation, met the president, and now here you are..." I pause. "Filming a homecoming special on national TV. With me. You must feel pretty blessed." I keep my face in deadpan. It has the effect I hoped, and Max lets out a deep laugh, and I smile. "Seriously, though, you've been through more than most people have in a lifetime. What are your plans for the future?"

"First, I want to kick my feet up far away from everything and relax. Then when I get bored of that, I'll get back out there."

"Where? Travel journalism?"

"Yes, but in a different way. I've received many letters from eager young men and women asking how to become a journalist. I plan to make it my mission to meet as many young people as I can who want to make this their career, especially the ones who are willing to risk their lives to find the truth. They need to know the reality of what they will be stepping into, but if they're like me, then nothing will stop them. There are a lot of stories that need honest, raw coverage from journalists with integrity and not just touting the company or network line."

Finally at the end of the interview, I wrap up, and we both relax back into the sofa when David finally yells that it's a wrap.

Reaching for my microphone, I stop when Karen tells me to keep it on. "We'd like you to be mic'ed for the party. We're setting up the book signing, and then you can walk around and mingle for a while before the dance."

"What book signing?" I ask.

"I set it up." Gillian stands, her velvet dress hangs heavy on her slight frame. "I thought it would be a good opportunity to meet your fans and have time face-to-face with them."

The last thing I feel like doing is being paraded around in a dog-and-pony show, but I don't want to let anyone down who's come out to meet me. It wouldn't be fair. But I still find it odd that some people consider me a (minor) celebrity.

As David and the crew are packing up, I pull Max aside. I'm not a proper journalist. I don't dig deep into a story, but when he mentioned that girl Jess, I know I grazed the top of something deeper. Even Gillian flinched.

"Now that the cameras are off, tell me about that soldier, Jessica Crossman. There's something more to that story."

Max looks alarmed and then recovers as he hooks the leash onto Bailey. "First, you tell me about Sam. I know there's something more to that story."

Touché.

He smiles, a twinkle in his eye. He knows he's got me. I doubt he knows the truth, but he's obviously a better reporter than I've given him credit for. He leaves, and I don't go after him.

Chapter 14
NATALIE

"What's Catie up to?" I ask, teetering toward Sam, who's on the velvety couch in the alcove of the lobby we've tucked into, waiting for Max and Catie to finish the interview. Two warm malt wines are cradled in the crook of my left elbow.

Sinking into the sofa, I wobble slightly, unable to balance with my right arm strapped to my side in a sling. Red liquid tips over the edge of one of the glasses, soaking into the black lace of my Nicole Miller gown. Correction. Catie's Nicole Miller gown.

"She's still doing the interview with Max."

"No, look. They finished. She's talking to some people near the reception desk." I dab at the stain on the delicate fabric, turning the white napkin crimson.

Leaning forward, Sam analyzes the scene. He's been uncharacteristically quiet since we left the townhouse. I expected him to be charming his way through the evening at the historic hotel. The ceiling soars above my head, accented with wood beams from an old ship; white garland is draped from the chair rail around the large lobby, and twinkling lights wink at us from the many surfaces covered in candles and tall vases of flowers. In his tailored gray suit, Sam looks like a present most of the ladies in the hotel lobby would want to unwrap. Everyone except Catie, who has been frostier than the ice hanging off the trees outside.

"She's signing books now." Sam yanks off his jacket and shoves the sleeves of his shirt up to his elbows.

"What?!" The floor is shaky under my feet as I stand. "I should be signing them. Half of what's between those pages belongs to me." I don't know if it's the wine, painkillers, jealousy, stupidity, or all of the above, but I've been in a volatile mood all night. Yes, yes, I agreed that Catie would take the credit for the book, but I still feel icky. Sam and I make a perfect pair with our fancy attire and sour attitudes. Every time the camera turns to my sister, sparks flare up inside me, making me want to tackle Catie to the ground and yank her hair like we did as kids when play turned rough.

"Slow down, Cowgirl. I don't think you'd be able to put pen to paper, even if you made it over there." Sam's hands are strong as he gently guides me back onto the plush sofa. For a moment, I consider sinking into the sofa next to this gorgeous man and just enjoying the festive atmosphere around us. But I can't.

Resting my chin on the edge of the sofa arm, I groan as Max pulls Catie away from the small gathering of fans and into the back of the spacious lobby next to a grand fireplace. The cameras follow them and David instructs from the sidelines. The music floats down from speakers above their heads, and Catie and Max begin to dance to some boring old standard.

When Max's hand moves to Catie's lower back and gently caresses it, my stomach clamps together, making me nauseous. How can my sister be such a ho-bag? She's married! Kind of.

"How did you know Catie wouldn't pull it off?"

Sam is scowling at Catie and Max as well, his eyes glued to them as they glide between the camera and the grand stone fireplace. "Huh?"

"The dinner. You must have ordered all that food to be catered a week ago."

"I didn't know she'd fail. It was a back-up plan. Just in case." Sam peels his eyes away from the dancing and stares into the small brick fireplace in front of him. Hot sparks pop from the logs like tiny firecrackers.

"How did you know the menu?"

"I looked at Catie's e-mail when she was out of her office."

"You little sneak."

Sam shrugs.

"How often have you snuck into her e-mail?"

"Just the once."

I try to cross my arms but fail. The drink and bound arm prevent it. But I convey the message with my eyes, and Sam looks sheepishly back to the fire.

"It's to protect her. I didn't want her to slip up with all the lies she's swimming in at the magazine."

"Why do you care?" I lock my eyes with his.

"I didn't want her to be fired."

He looks back at the dancing couple and then softens as he takes my sister in. Catie's crimson dress presses tight around her body, hugging every part of her. Her hair is piled on top of her head in a messy bun, accentuating her long neck. As the dance ends, Max slides Catie into a dip and lowers his face to hers.

"Get your hands off her!" Sam knocks the wine glass at his feet over as he charges forward. Seeing no other choice, I tackle him around the ankles with one arm and we both land hard on the floor, falling on my left side. Rolling over, we lay on our stomachs, watching Max kiss Catie's cheek. The alcove is tucked away at the far end of the lobby—no one seems to have noticed our skirmish.

"If I can't stir up trouble, neither can you." As I crawl back to the sofa, my arm aches from the fall. I look back at the dance floor and see that others have joined Max and Catie now, but they don't seem to have noticed—they have eyes only for each other. Next to me, Sam's fists are gripping the edge of the sofa. The wine sours in my stomach. Max has pulled Catie closer and they both have gag-worthy grins on their faces. I want to punch both of them.

Gillian marches over to the couch. "Mr. Harding, I need to speak to you."

Sam's eyes stay locked on Catie and Max.

"Harding!"

"Oh, Ms. Kennedy. Sorry, ma'am." Quickly coming to his feet, Sam follows Gillian, his head down like a schoolboy in trouble.

There's a small podium and microphone next to the stone fireplace that dominates the center of the lobby. Watching Max spin Catie around in his arms, I'm sick of being the silent partner. Maybe if Max knew the truth, that Catie is a fraud, he wouldn't be so enchanted by her. It's time to give a little speech in honor of my little sister.

Finding the on switch, I hit the top of the microphone with two fingers, creating a loud thud. An older couple near the reception desk turn, but most people stay engrossed in their own conversations.

Bringing the microphone close to my lips, I yell, "Hey. Hey!"

Curious eyes from around the room and bar turn to me. It is overflowing on this Saturday evening.

"Good evening, everyone. I'm Catie...er, Catelyn Bloom's sister, Natalie. Not that anyone would even know that she has a sister. But anyway, um...I wanted to say how proud I am of all the stuff she's accomplished. It's amazing how someone with such a big social and work life in the city can also have time for the perfect home life: cooking three-course gourmet meals and being the perfect homemaker and wife to boot. But as you all fawn over her, admiring her accomplishments, there's something you should know. Catie isn't—"

The microphone is ripped out of my hand, causing me to stumble backward and land on my rump. Fifty pairs of eyes are staring at me, dumbstruck, while Sam, who is now holding the microphone, glares at me. Then he turns on his thousand-watt smile and addresses the crowd.

"Thank you, Natalie. Your sister is amazing, and she does lead a full life, and no one is more proud of her than me. As her..." Sam's attention is caught by a commotion at the edge of the lobby. The older couple from reception is waving at him. "Uh...uh..." Recovering, he continues, but his voice struggles to find solid ground.

"As...um, she reminds me every day, her overnight success took ten years of hard work. So here's to Catelyn Bloom, the woman who works hard to make all of our lives easier."

There's a scattering of applause that dies quickly as I'm lifted off the floor and flung over Sam's shoulder like a rolled up rug. "I thought you wanted to put her in her place as much as I did?" I hiss into his backside. "Why the hell—"

Sam slings me off his shoulder to a standing position, gripping my injured arm with just enough force to shut me up as we come face to face with the couple who was waving to Sam.

"Mom. Dad. What are you doing here?"

"Sammy, honey, you never miss your birthday dinner with us, and when you mentioned you were coming to this hotel tonight, your father and I wanted to surprise you." His mother gives Sam a long embrace. "Your father says I'm overreacting, but you were so vague about your plans. I thought something was wrong."

"You should have called."

"We did, but your phone's off," Sam's father says. He has a thick head of shockingly white hair and looks like an older version of his son. He turns to me. "I'm Adam Harding, and this is my wife, Lily."

"I'm Natalie. Nice to meet you."

The smart-looking couple wears matching black-and-white semiformal attire and look like chess pieces. The smiles on their faces are wide and friendly, but his mother keeps looking over at Catie. Does she suspect something? "Oh, look! There's Catie. Sammy, introduce us. You're always so cagey about her, though you talk about her nonstop."

"She's busy filming."

"How do you know Sammy?" Mrs. Harding moves her gaze over my dress and rests her eyes on my arm in a sling.

"Through Catie. She's my sister."

"Oh, right. I heard your little speech over there." The look on Mrs. Harding's face suggests she thinks I took the short bus to school. "Are you helping with the TV special?"

The sound of Catie's heels reverberating off the wood floor as she marches toward us draws my attention. From the other side of the room, Gillian is making a beeline for our little group too. The desire to blow Catie's world apart has quickly dissipated, and my heart is skittering in my chest at the oncoming collision.

"Is that Gillian Kennedy? Can we meet her too?"

"No!" Sam and I both yell.

"I mean, everything is so hectic. Why don't I take you both to the bar to get a drink?" Sam shifts his eyes to Catie, who steps away from us. He doesn't have enough time to make the escape. "Catelyn, darling!" Snatching her hand, he smashes his lips into her cheek and gives her owl eyes, indicating she needs to shut up, and then speaks overly brightly. "These are my parents, Adam and Lily Harding. My mom is a big fan."

As Gillian arrives, all anger disappears from Catie's face as she converts to her role of gracious hostess. "How lovely to meet you both."

"Good, I'm glad you're both here." Gillian's large tote almost knocks me over as she turns toward Catie. "I need to speak to your husband about a few details regarding his new position, which involves you too, Ms. Bloom."

"Husband?" Mrs. Harding's expression is incredulous as she looks for rings on both their hands—a little detail everyone seems to have missed until this moment. "Honey, what is she talking about?"

Mrs. Harding's face looks so crushed that I want to tell her the truth right then and there.

"We must have a cover story about the two of you. Everyone will fall in love with the simply chic couple. The homemaker and the sports writer. America will swoon." Gillian pats Sam on the back. "You've been very quiet about your talented husband. But that is about to change."

The smile on Catie's face falters.

"What is she talking about?" Mrs. Harding looks imploringly at Sam.

"Ms. Kennedy, what a great idea. Let's discuss it where it's quieter." Sam guides Gillian away from the group.

"What's going on?" Mrs. Harding's chest has red splotches on it, and her breathing is coming out in short gasps. "Sam isn't married. I would know. He would tell me."

"Natalie, get her some water," Catie orders, taking Mrs. Harding's hand in hers, but Mr. Harding has already poured a glass from the pitcher on a table nearby and hands it to his wife.

After two large gulps, she asks, "Are you married to our son?"

"No! No. Of course not. We just had to tell Gillian we are. It was a little white lie that got out of hand."

"What about your husband?" Mrs. Harding releases her hand from Catie's and steps back. "From your columns?"

"That's the problem." Catie bites her lip and looks at me for help, but I have nothing. My mind is blank. "Things aren't going so well between my husband and me, and Gillian would fire me if she found out that America's happy homemaker is getting a divorce, so Sam stepped in."

"You poor girl."

Another day. Another lie. I'm amazed how easily they roll off my sister's tongue.

Released from Mrs. Harding's embrace, Catie pulls her aside. "I'm absolutely in love with your dress. Could I persuade you and your dress to be photographed for the magazine's fashion blog?"

The husband debacle is quickly forgotten, and they scurry away as Catie beckons one of the hired photographers to their side. Mr. Harding, who has looked a little shell shocked through all the commotion, wanders after his wife.

"We'll finish this discussion in the morning, and I'll have contracts drawn up by the New Year," Gillian is saying as she and Sam rejoin me. With a quick shake, Gillian bids us a good night. "'Early to bed and early to rise makes a man healthy, wealthy, and wise.' Ben Franklin."

The air lightens when Gillian's imposing presence exits the lobby, but the weariness inside my bones takes over. I drag my feet as I walk back to the alcove. Collapsing on the sofa again, I kick my feet up and close my eyes.

"What the hell was that?" Before I can drift off blissfully into dreamland, Catie is hissing in my ear, making me wish I had finished my little speech on the stage earlier. Behind her, Sam is barreling toward us.

"Huh? I'm a little loopy right now. The drugs."

"Bullshit. You know exactly what I'm talking about. Your little stunt over there." She indicates the podium. "If it weren't for Sam coming to the rescue, we'd all be ruined."

"None of that matters now that Gillian is hell bent on doing a cover story on us." Sam snaps his rolled up sleeves down and wrestles his arms back into his suit jacket. Two young women in their early twenties wearing black minidresses strut by, eyeing Sam like a lollipop they want to lick.

Catie blocks their view and lowers her voice. "We'll refuse."

"Like you refused to do this special?"

Red splotches creep up Catie's neck, a sign she's angry but has no smart rebuttal. Catie hates nothing more than losing an argument, especially something personal. "You obviously think you could have done better. Now's your chance to prove me wrong."

"I don't want to prove you wrong. I want to keep my job and be done with this whole mess," Sam says.

"Gillian can't make us do the cover story. Besides, she already knows you're camera shy. We'll just play that up. Tell her you don't want to be in the spotlight." Taking a deep breath, Catie pulls her lipstick from her clutch and slowly spreads crimson over her plump lips. "Now, if you'll excuse me, I need to find Max."

"You're married. You can't have him," I blurt out, my head fuzzy with images of Max's hand on my sister's waist as they danced.

"Don't you get it? I *know* I can't have him. Ever!" Hair has come loose from Catie's bun, and the strands are bobbing up and down with the clipped cadence of her voice. "I'm going to be on national TV playing the perfect domestic goddess and hostess to Max Euston, the nation's latest media darling. What am I going to do? Run off with him the next week? A cheating wife is not someone other women want to take advice from."

The fire flickers higher, and the music from the speakers blares the latest pop hit. The red-orange glow from the flames moves across Catie's face, distorting her features.

"Have you guys forgotten that you're the ones who cooked up this whole charade? I was ready to throw in the towel after that doomed meeting with Gillian and Charles. But you both convinced me to do this. You practically begged me." The flames seem to flicker faster as Catie bats her hand in front of her face.

"Don't throw this on us. We're doing everything to save your ass, and you're being an ungrateful..." He halts, shoving his hands through his hair. His eyes are fierce, filled with anger. Or passion. There's an undercurrent to the fight that feels like a lover's quarrel. No one gets this angry unless they have more than just their jobs at stake.

"Bitch." Catie finishes, her eyes challenging him to deny the word that was about to escape his lips. "It's good to know how far your opinion of me has dropped."

"Stop playing the victim. You could have said no. We didn't force you. Your choices are your own."

"I'm so sick of your self-righteous superiority and constant judgment, Sam. No one's making you stay either. You want this to be over? Fine. Where's Gillian? Gillian!" Catie marches through the throngs of people that are gathered in front of the grand fireplace near the center of the room. "Gillian!"

Sam and I scurry after her, reaching out to grab her.

Catie takes out her phone. "I'll call her." The phone is snatched out of her fingers, and Sam pockets it. "Isn't this what you want, Sam? I'm trying to do the right thing. Aren't I being the girl you fell in love with? Isn't this what you were yelling about the other night? My integrity?"

Turning on her red patent-leather heels, Catie stumbles back through the oblivious revelers who have become sloppy by this late hour. Her hair comes loose and tumbles around her shoulders as she swings around and smacks into a man drinking from a flask. He doesn't seem to notice and continues drinking.

When Catie reaches the lobby doors, she is intercepted by David and Karen who huddle around her, their lips moving rapidly. Catie shakes her head, indicating her hair and pointing toward Sam and me.

Shoulders hunched, Catie follows behind David as he approaches us, the smell of sweat, BO, and grease wafting from him, reminding me of a college dorm room. He may not have slept all weekend with their hectic schedule.

"They need one last shot before we can wrap." Catie's arms are crossed as tight as a straitjacket across her chest as she directs her comment to Sam.

"What shot?" Sam squints as a light from one of the cameras is directed at him.

"Us. The happy couple dancing."

David motions to Karen, directing the shot, as lights are positioned around the dance floor.

"No. They can't film me," Sam insists.

Looking over at the parquet floor in front of the fireplace that has turned into a dance floor, David says, "We need a shot of Ms. Bloom with her husband. You can be dancing with your back to camera. And we'll grab another shot of you two in the morning at the breakfast table. Again, just from behind. Otherwise, it looks like Ms. Bloom has been hosting Max and Ms. Kennedy alone. We didn't get many useable shots of you during the dinner."

"Fine."

The tension between Sam and Catie is tangible, and as David looks them over, he scratches his head, concerned.

"Did you two have a fight?"

"Yes," Sam says as she blurts, "no."

"It doesn't matter. Just get through one song, and we'll be out of here." David stifles a yawn, obviously not caring if the soon-to-be America's sweethearts aren't being so sweet. But Sam and Catie haven't budged.

"My crew and I have been working on very little sleep for the past forty-eight hours, we've barely seen our families, and we'd really like to call it a night. So, if you don't mind."

Chagrined, Catie takes Sam's hand, and they walk onto the dance floor among a small sea of happy couples floating on the bubbles of the libations they've been drinking all night.

Stillness wraps around me as everyone departs. I'm finally alone, but a presence near the bar draws my attention. Max. He shoves his hands into his pockets as he watches Catie and Sam dancing. I catch his eye, and he walks toward me and stands, still watching the dance floor.

"Where have you been?" I ask.

"I was trying to call someone but couldn't get through."

"Who were you calling?"

"I need to get out of here." Not waiting for an answer, he walks away. I hurry after him.

"Wait. I'll come too. I've had enough merriment for one night."

I almost ram into Max as he stops in his tracks. "Stay here. I don't want company."

The bit of joy that had been running through my body disappears as I watch Max retreat. I thought his vigil in my room while I slept off the painkillers last night had somehow bonded us, but I was wrong.

A feeling of hopelessness drops into my chest as Max disappears from sight. I didn't realize I wanted him until right now, when he's made it clear he doesn't want me.

Chapter 15

CATIE

The wood floor is sticky under my red heels, which adds to the awkwardness between Sam and me as we dance. Taming my hair with my free hand, I glance at David, who is behind one of the cameras, directing us.

"Give me my phone."

When Sam doesn't budge, I reach my hand into his pocket and pull it out.

"What are you doing?" His mouth is caught between a frown and a grin.

"Taking matters into my own hands."

He laughs, and I can feel his anger thaw.

Opening the camera function, I reapply my red lipstick and put everything back into my clutch, tucking it in a chair beside the fireplace. As the music fades into a modern rendition of "Feeling Good"—one of my favorites—David signals that they're rolling.

I slide my left hand around Sam's back, my fingers pressing into the warmth of his skin that I can feel through his crisp shirt as we sway together. The back of my dress is low and his fingers move over my bare skin. The tiny caresses from his fingers send electric shocks down into my thighs, making me light headed and disoriented.

It didn't used to be like this. I could've danced a thousand dances with Sam before this weekend and never been this disjointed. I've never denied that Sam is hot. He's all broad shouldered, tall, muscled, the perfect specimen of a man, with hair you want to feel between your fingers and eyes that capture you with a glance. I've been able to deny my attraction to him for years, but something happened in that room when he confessed his feelings. As much as I want to reject what he said, I'm a total sucker for those three words. I haven't heard them since...since college. Now they've unhinged me, as if gravity doesn't exist, and I've been lifted from the ground, losing all sense of who I am.

This isn't me. I don't let a man rule my emotions or my life. If he hadn't confessed his damn feelings for me I'd be fine. *Fine!* My mind is screaming, *Stay away!* But my body betrays me, begging to get lost in every fiber of his being. I'm fighting it, but as the tender melody of the song spins its way inside me, it breaks my will.

I lean into Sam, and I'm grateful when he pulls me close, my head falling to his shoulder. All at once, the knot that gripped my insides releases, and I soften into his arms, the warmth of his body flowing into mine. Tears pop into my eyes, and I squeeze them shut until the wetness disappears.

What the hell has gotten into me? I've always been cool under pressure. Emotions are easy to tame; if they pop up, push them down.

Focus, girl! Let's remember the objective of this weekend. I love my life. I love my career. I love my new apartment. I don't want to lose it. Any of it.

The metronome of Sam's heart thumping against my chest pulls me back down and calms my racing mind. *Chris.* The name flashes in my mind, and I tense. There's something about this moment that has brought the memory of my ex to

143

the forefront of my mind. Despite everything, Sam's arms around me make me feel safe, and the last time I was lulled into the safety net of love, it destroyed me in a way that has kept my heart in a vice. Love is a minefield of hurt and humiliation, which I've avoided since Chris blew me apart.

Christophe Martine and I worked in the same dumpy coffee shop during my junior year of college, when I was going through my pink-haired, I'm-a-liberal-artist phase, and his extracurricular activity was pursuing me. He made up a game—Did it, Dissed, or Too Drunk to Get It Up—when couples would stagger into the coffee shop. The morning shift was brutal, but watching hungover co-eds stumble in and deciphering their nocturnal activities with Chris made me eager to get to work. Soon, I was ditching classes to hang out with him. We'd go on impromptu field trips into the city for a new art exhibit or to a local winery for free tastings or trivia night at a bar. After several months of these outings, we were inseparable, and I fell in love with him. Hard.

As we tumbled into love, Chris's mother was diagnosed with breast cancer. It was stage two, but she needed several months of chemo and a mastectomy. Chris was from a small village outside Bordeaux, France, called Agen. He had to drop out of school and return home for six months as his mother went through the therapy and surgery. I visited and helped out that summer and grew close to his mother. She was eager to see her son settle down, but we laughed it off, since we were only twenty-one at the time.

When she was finally in the clear, Chris came back to school, and we were connected on a much deeper level after everything we'd been through with his mother. But Chris had flown into the country on a tourist visa and applied to renew his student visa, but it was denied since he'd dropped out of school the previous semester. We were both crushed. I was so crazy in love that I couldn't let him go. When he suggested we get married, I didn't hesitate, and within the month, it was done. We flew to Vegas, got the marriage license, did the whole married with Elvis in the little white wedding chapel, and flew back.

Then everything changed. Chris became distant and mean. Any time I tried to talk to him about it, he yelled at me and made me feel small and stupid. I assumed he was going through some delayed grieving and anger for what had happened to his mother. He'd been so involved in her caretaking that he didn't have time to deal with his own emotions. I would have told myself anything to believe he still loved me, but the truth came out one night when he stumbled back from the bars with his friends, where he spent most his nights.

He'd been spending a lot of time with the international students, telling me I wouldn't understand with my small, brainwashed American mind. Only other foreigners could understand him and his life in this country. When he came home that night, he'd been high on cocaine and was nastier than usual. Typically, he was quiet and depressed. I assumed it was part of being French. But the drugs made him manic and mean.

He started packing his things, telling me he was moving out. I begged him to stay, told him over and over how much I loved him. When all his clothes were shoved into the back of his black Jetta, he turned to me and told me he didn't love me, he had never loved me, and had only used me for a visa.

I believed him. I believed every word. I was so in love with him when he said those words—they crippled me. I didn't understand how I could be so blind. He had to love me. I couldn't believe I'd been that big a fool. But I must have been, because he left and never came back to me.

I was so crushed and discombobulated that it was a year before I realized he'd never filed divorce papers. After I graduated, still no papers arrived, and it made me wonder if he'd really meant all those awful things he said. Maybe he regretted leaving me and couldn't bring himself to sever that last connection to me. It also meant he hadn't met anyone else. At least, no one he wanted to marry. It gave me a warped sense of comfort knowing he'd never remarried.

Until two weeks ago. When a manila envelope arrived with divorce papers. Attached to the papers was a smaller white envelope with a letter inside with my name in Chris's scratchy handwriting. I couldn't bring myself to read it. It's in my suitcase. At the last minute, I grabbed it, unsure why. Maybe to torture myself. Or maybe I felt by the end of this crazy weekend the letter wouldn't seem so scary. But it still sits in the inside zipper of my suitcase. Unread.

"The music stopped."

Sam's low voice startles me. We're still dancing, but the cameras have stopped rolling. My mind is slowly unwrapping from my memories, but my emotions are back in those days so long ago.

David and the crew are dragging their equipment out the side door to the van, the dog hopping along next to them, and there is only a scattering of people left in the lobby.

"What are you thinking about?"

"Chris," I say.

Sam's back muscles tighten under my hand.

"He's getting married. At least, I think he is."

Sam lifts my chin, and his eyes hold mine. "What he did to you in college is not okay."

Sam knows about my relationship with Chris and how he jilted me. He doesn't know we were, and still are, married.

"It's more complicated than you realize."

"He was cruel and toxic. Don't ever question that. You deserve—" Sam halts our dancing. "You deserve better than the way that asshole treated you."

His face is shrouded with certainty as his hands grip me tighter, urging me to hear his words, to make me understand that I am worthy of love from someone honest and good.

Moments ago, he was righteously telling me off; now he's trying to comfort and care for me. I can't take this Jekyll-and-Hyde relationship anymore. Sam isn't trying to hurt or manipulate me, but our back-and-forths are exhausting, and when he looks at me like this, I think he might really care about me. But I have no idea if I can trust his feelings. With the music and the charade we're playing and this dress and his hands on me, we're fooling ourselves into false emotions.

As I peel myself off him, a chill runs over my skin where his body no longer touches mine. "Thanks for the dance."

"Wait, Catie. I—"

"I'm tired of this game, Sam. I don't want to play anymore. I know what you think of me and my life and career choices. I get it. Can we just leave it for now? I don't want to fight anymore. And I don't want to make up. I just want to be."

The softness in his eyes disappears. "We need to talk."

"I'm tired." I grab my clutch and hold it tight to my chest.

"Gillian wants to make me editor in chief of her new extreme-sports magazine."

"I know. That's great, Sam. I guess you did get something out of this weekend."

"No, Catie. It means I'll be fired."

"What are you talking about?"

"I told you, she's only promoting me because you're my wife. She thinks having the husband of Catelyn Bloom behind this new venture will launch it into a bigger spotlight. She wants to make our so-called relationship very public and is toting us as the new 'it' couple in our little media world. She's even pitching Charles a reality show."

"Did you tell Gillian no?"

"Gillian doesn't hear no."

"I'll figure it out. I'll get you out of it."

"Forget it. Every time you try to help, you make it worse."

Max, who I haven't spoken to since we danced earlier, is walking across the lobby toward us.

"I'll get you out of it. I promise. Even if I have to—"

"Shut up, and listen to me, Catie." The tone of Sam's voice isn't mean; it's filled with frustration. "Don't do anything. You were right before. I'm the idiot who volunteered to be part of this mess. I'll find my own way to fix it. Without you."

"Hi, Max!" I say brightly as he approaches, covering the pain I feel. "Where did you run off to?"

"Had to answer a quick call." A few drops of liquid run down the side of the copper mug Max grips. He holds it out to me. "Moscow Mule. You look like you need it."

I take the proffered drink, guzzling the crisp liquid. Max's presence is warm and cracks the sheet of ice Sam has thrown over me. "I need a walk. Want to join me?"

As we exit the lobby, I see Natalie approach Sam. My head is still spinning. We're so close to the finish line. Why did Gillian have to come and mess it all up? Not that I can really blame her. If Sam and I really were married, I'd be jumping at this opportunity. Gillian's not stupid.

Stepping outside under the red awning, I'm overwhelmed by the twinkling lights dangling from the trim of the awning and the thin layer of snow brushed over the quiet street. It's early in the season for snow. It sprinkles me with a bit of wintery magic, and my insides warm. I forgot how much I love snow, when it's still fresh and white, before the cars and pedestrians turn it into a dingy, gray slush.

"Freedom." Max's eyes droop slightly, and his smile is crooked as he watches the TV van drive away from the hotel. "Even when they're not filming, I felt like I needed to perform." He touches the pine needles of an overhanging tree limb and brings his fingers to his nose. "Pine always smells like Christmas to me and reminds me of a thousand things. I had a good childhood. It wasn't perfect, but it was good." A group of tuxedoed men push through the lobby doors, cigars hanging from their mouths, laughing in low voices. "Is Natalie still here?"

"She's probably getting drunk with Sam." And talking smack about me. "I'm sure they'll have a fabulous time together."

"Doesn't that bother you?"

"No. They can do whatever they want. They're both sin—" I catch myself just in time, sucking the word *single* back in—"er, having fun."

Max's cheeks are flushed, and he looks a little dizzy.

"Are you okay?"

His fingers massage his temples. "All the dancing and festivities...sometimes I still get nauseous."

The cigar-smoking men are on the other side of the entrance, their gravely voices ebbing and flowing. Clouds have covered the full moon, but the streetlights create a soft glow around us. There's a bench to the right of the entrance, and we sit. A shiver runs through my body as my back makes contact with the cold metal.

Pulling something from beneath him, Max wraps a fur blanket around my shoulders. Seeing the two sleeves dangling at the side, I realize it's a coat. I push my arms through and snuggle into the warmth. "I guess someone left it."

We sit for a while, swept away by the quiet beauty of the night, the lights twinkling around us. The air is heavy and still, ready for the next snowfall, and the thought of Sam and our dance isn't leaving me as quickly as I'd hoped. The dynamics of our relationship changed so quickly, my head hurts. *Okay, fine. It's my heart that hurts. I admit it!* I hate that his feelings for me have shifted from love to distaste. Ever since I've known him, he's been all flattery and flirtatious. Of course, I never took it too seriously because he was that way with everyone.

At least, I thought he was. He's certainly a charmer, but it's *my* desk he always comes to. It's *me* he always takes to lunch for so-called business meetings. Could he really have been wooing me this whole time? I mean, seriously wooing me? I thought I was just another trophy he was trying to win, but maybe I was the grand prize he's been after this whole time. I miss the old Sam. The man who ruthlessly flirted with me and made me feel special.

"Let's play pretend," I say.

Max leans his head back, closing his eyes. "Okay."

"Let's pretend we just met."

"We did just meet."

"Pretend you don't know who I am. If you saw me across a room, would you flirt with me?"

"No."

I sit up and look at him.

He laughs, his eyes still shut. "I can feel your indignation. I wouldn't flirt with you because I'd be too intimidated."

"Oh." I lean back, relaxing.

"Why does Natalie call you Little Bee?"

Hearing the familiar name makes my chin quiver. I hadn't thought about the origin of the name in years. But it came from me always buzzing around her when I was little. I never left her side until I started school. Instead, I say, "I don't deserve a pet name. They're for people who're loved."

"Aren't you loved?"

"I guess I'm just feeling sorry for myself."

"Sometimes it's nice to be self indulgent."

"Okay, I'll sit here and wallow in my misery."

Max laughs again. "I enjoyed dancing with you tonight, Little Bee."

A smile touches my lips as I hear the thousand times Natalie has spoken that name. I thought I hated the nickname, but it makes me feel all warm and fuzzy.

"I like it when you smile." Max's eyes are studying me, looking from my face down to my hands clasped tightly in my lap.

"I'm not sure I have much to smile about right now."

"Look!" Max jumps from the bench. "It's snowing again."

I follow him as he stands. My inner child is jumping up and down, and suddenly nothing seems as worrisome as it did a moment ago. We run down the road and stand under a street lamp, watching the snowflakes fall in the light.

"It's so magical, isn't it?"

"You make it magical," Max says.

"Flattery will get you everywhere." I slide my arm through the crook of Max's elbow, and we walk toward an enclosed playground on the corner.

The snow is falling faster, the flakes melting on my face. I swipe at them and sit on the cold metal seat of a seesaw, hiking my dress up. Max sits across from me. My feet press into the hard soil and soft snow, and I float high above the ground.

"You seem upset." Max shoves his legs, sending me floating down as he sits high above me. "Is it something I said?"

"Oh, no. It's something I did. Or didn't do."

"What?"

"Sometimes you dig a hole so deep, you can't even see the light anymore." Pushing my feet down, I float up again, my legs dangling in the air, the snow falling faster.

"Are you talking about your marriage?"

"Bring me down," I say, in lieu of an answer.

"Not until you answer my question."

I grasp the tiny seat under me, the ground looking miles away. I'm not even sure which marriage is worrying me right now—the one that made me into the hard-hearted woman that I am, or the fake one that is slowly chipping away at the hardness.

"My marriage is a mess, but not in the way you think." Here I am with this gorgeous man as the snow falls around us in the most romantic way, and I can't get Sam or the rest of my life out of my mind. "Sam is infuriating. He acts all noble and caring, but I ask one favor of him, and suddenly he thinks I've ruined his life. When I first met him, he was a total womanizer. At least, that's what he led me to believe. If only he could have told me the truth instead of being a coward and hiding behind his charm and ego. But then he turned his whole life upside for me and was completely unselfish, and I couldn't see past my own agenda to realize he has this huge heart, and he's actually very giving. And now it's too late."

The words have tumbled out of my mouth, and I'm not sure what I've said.

"The air's a bit thin up here," I joke.

Max slowly lowers me down. We balance for a moment, looking at each other. "You're in love with him."

I jump off, causing Max to fall. "No! Er...I mean, of course I am." I force a laugh. "He's my husband."

"I found them!"

At the sharp voice, I turn to see a short rotund woman in a green-velvet gown standing at the edge of the playground.

"Excuse me?" I look behind me, wondering whom she's referring to.

"That's my coat." The woman indicates the fur coat I'm still wearing.

Max and I exchange a glance.

"Sorry, I found it on a bench." I slip it off.

"Bill!" the woman yells down the street.

"She wasn't going to keep it. We just got excited by the snow." Max steps next to me, the snow blanketing us.

"Bill! Hurry!"

Suddenly, a not-so-jolly plump man appears, his face red and his eyes sloshing in his head, not quite focusing on us.

"These people have my coat!"

The man narrows his eyes and lunges for us. I drop the coat and step back, avoiding the man's clumsy attack.

"Run!" Max yells.

We race down the street, until we're lost—in our laughter, in the streets of Brooklyn, and into the night.

Chapter 16
NATALIE

 " "I've called Catie's phone and left three messages." I plop on top of the bed in Sam and Catie's room, my insides twisting in knots thinking of Max out with Catie all night, holding her hand, kissing her lips, falling in love with her. For a moment, earlier today, I thought Max might like me, but we left the hotel hours ago, and Max and Catie are nowhere to be found.

"I looked all over the house. They aren't here." Sam moves to the dresser, pouring us both a scotch. I hate scotch, but at this point I'd lick the bottom of a shoe if it would make this sick feeling go away. "I stole it from the hotel bar."

"I shouldn't mix any more alcohol with the medication. I've already had too much." I slug the whole drink down. Closing my eyes, I wait for the warm blanket of liquor to wrap around my brain, blurring out the images. I didn't realize how much I liked Max until he disappeared with Catie.

"Do you think they're…" Sam trails off.

"Let's not go there." The plush rug will soon be bare from Sam's pacing. I close my eyes. "Knock it off. You're making me sick."

"Catie makes me sick." The mattress sags as Sam falls onto the bed; his weight makes me roll toward him.

"That's what love does." My fingers touch his arm soothingly. The frustration in his eyes fades for a moment and is replaced by sad resignation.

"Stop saying that." His eyes close tightly.

My heart aches for his pain. The crush I have on Max is fledgling; it hurts, but I'll be over it in a week. To be in love with someone and to know they want someone else crushes your soul. The weight of it suffocates your spirit, and all you're left with is an empty, sad shell you'd do anything to rip off, but you can't. It sticks to you, not letting you breath or be yourself or live your life freely. You become its slave.

There were many times I watched Sam with Catie, flirting and flattering and teasing, but he kept it light. There were moments I thought he might have genuine feelings for my sister; he threw an anti-Valentine's Day party, and Catie was the only one who showed up—or as I now suspect, she was the only one Sam actually invited—or when we were all in Barnes and Noble, killing time before a birthday party near Union Square, and Sam moved all of Catie's books onto a display table when he thought no one was looking. And at their company Christmas party last year, he got Catie's date so wasted that the date mistook the supply closet for a toilet. Sam said it was an accident, but I knew it wasn't.

Our faces are an inch apart as we lie sprawled on the bed, making Sam's eyes appear as one cyclopean eye. I push my head back. Sam's lazy eyes search my face. "You have her eyes."

My head is growing cloudy from the drink, and I move my good hand up and down his muscled forearm, tracing his silky veins with my fingers. "You have his arms."

Closing my eyes, I imagine Max under my touch, the warmth of his blood pulsing beneath my fingers, increasing the heat in my own bloodstream. I lean forward, and my lips find his, soft and eager. Those strong arms pull me close as I kiss him more frantically.

"Oh, Catie."

"Oh, Max."

My head is gently pulled back, and I groan, wanting the kiss to continue. As I flutter my eyes open, my body jolts. Sam's face stares back at me, his eyes blinking rapidly. We fall into each other, fits of laughter rippling through both of us.

"Oh my God. We're so pathetic." Sam's sad amusement matches mine.

A movement across the room catches my attention. I freeze. Catie is standing in the doorway with her hand over her gaping mouth. A moment later, Max is by her side, taking in the tangled limbs and rumpled sheets.

"What the hell?" Max looks at everyone, trying to sort out the scene.

Catie storms at Sam. "Hypocrite! You make me feel guilty for *almost* kissing someone, and here you are in bed with my sister! Why?"

The expression on Catie's face begs for a reasonable explanation, but Sam stays on the bed, staring at Catie, nonplussed.

"Where have you two been for the past three hours?"

"Don't change—" Catie starts.

But Max interrupts. "Lost."

"Lost?" I repeat.

"It started with a misunderstanding. Not that either of you care. You've been in here making out like horny teenagers."

"That's her husband!" Max comes to Catie's defense.

Oh, God, this must look really bad to him.

"Now you care about her husband?!" I yell back, pointing a finger at Max. "Did you care the other night when you kissed her?"

"I didn't kiss her."

"You would've kissed her if I hadn't interrupted." Now Sam is standing, the muscles in his face tight. The four of us form a tight circle, voices high and faces red.

"What do you care?" Catie yells at Sam. "Oh, wait, sorry, you do care. Oh, no, just kidding. You don't care."

"Yes, we almost kissed," Max says. "But it was a mistake. We both agree. Right?"

"Yes."

Turning to Sam, Max puts out his hand. "I'm sorry, man. I shouldn't have done that."

Smacking Max's hand away, Sam knocks him slightly off balance, and I automatically move to Max. "Why the hell did you do that? You know Catie was the one pursuing Max. And it's not like Max actually did anything wrong."

When I touch Max's shoulder, he brushes me off.

"You're mad at *me*?" I demand.

"Yes."

"Why?"

"Because I..." Max looks lost for a moment. "Because you were kissing her husband. That's just...it's wrong."

"Screw you!" I push Max aside, sending pain up my injured arm.

"I'm not the one making out with a married man!" Max yells back.

"No, you're trying to make out with a married woman!"

"No, I'm not!" The fury in his voice makes me pause. "You people have it so good." Sucking air in through his nose, Max breathes out low and steady. "You have families that love you and beautiful homes and careers that you actually like. You live in a privileged society. You don't have to worry about anything. Traveling around the globe, I see how the rest of the world lives, and for the most part, it's not like this. There's a lot more struggle and grief and pain. But you all have family and friends who support and love you.

And you can't even appreciate it because you're all so spoiled."

Max has been so laidback and quiet that I almost forgot who he is and where he comes from. Besides Charles and Gillian, who haven't exactly been the doting aunt and uncle, he has no one. No wonder he travels all over the world. He has no home. And here we are, bickering like children.

"When you put it that way." My attempt at a joke falls flat. Max is right. We are all selfish, spoiled brats.

"I'm going to the bathroom, and then I'm going to bed." Max walks into the en suite and closes the door to the toilet behind him.

I collapse onto the sofa in front of the tall windows, exhausted from the events of the night.

"Happy?" Sam shoots at Catie.

"Yes! I'm elated," Catie shoots back, her hands flying up in the air. "This is exactly how I hoped this weekend would turn out. Everyone miserable and the guest of honor disgusted by all of us." It looks like Catie is going to continue her tirade, but she sinks onto the sofa next to me, staring out the window. When I follow her gaze, I see that Catie is staring at her own image reflecting back from the dark windowpanes. "I've made a mess of everything. You both think I'm selfish and blinded by my career, screwing over anyone in my path. I didn't mean for it to be that way. I was trying to help save everyone's asses, including my own." The wind bangs against the panes, shaking Catie's reflection. "I can't do this. I can't let them air this special. I can't bring Max—sweet, innocent, broken Max—down with me. I have to talk to Gillian. Now."

When Catie marches to the door and opens it, there's a woman about my age standing on the other side, her fist raised as if she were about to knock, a tan duffel bag in one hand. What must have once been a pageboy cut hangs long and unkempt around the woman's narrow face. Her shoulders are held back and straight, reminding me of Max's often-stilted stance. The brown eyes that stare into the room at us are wide and bright, but the lids hang heavy.

"Sorry. I knocked downstairs, but no one answered, so I came in. This was the only light I saw on in the house. I was meant to arrive hours ago." When no one speaks, the woman continues. "I'm looking for Max Euston. Gillian Kennedy invited me. I would have been here much earlier, but my train was delayed by the storm in DC."

"Come in." Catie finally finds her voice and opens the door wider. "Max is in the bathroom." She indicates the doors across the room.

"I thought he'd be asleep, but Max never sleeps." The tan duffel bag she carries, similar to the one Max arrived with, falls from her hands with a *thump*. "I'm sorry if I woke you."

"We were awake. I don't mean to be rude, but who are you?" Catie asks.

"I'm sorry. I should have said. I'm just so tired. I've been traveling for the past seventy-two hours." The woman puts out her hand, and Catie shakes it. I'm already anticipating what's about to come. "I'm Jessica Crossman. Max's fiancé."

Chapter 17
NATALIE

"Jess?" Max is standing in the middle of the room, his face a mix of confusion and joy. "I thought you weren't coming until tomorrow?"

"Your aunt called and asked if I could come a day early. She wanted me to surprise you while you were shooting the special but then the weather delayed everything." Max walks to Jess, and his lips press to hers. I have a sudden urge to yank their faces apart. "I'm on leave for the next month." Jess pauses. "There was an IED." Max's eyes widen, and he stills. "Don't worry. There were some injuries, but everyone's going to be okay."

There's an intimacy between them that makes me feel silly about the way I acted earlier. "Excuse me, I need to—"

"How long have you two been engaged?" Sam interrupts me. Catie stands beside him, still in her red-sequined gown. She looks stunning—disheveled and flustered but stunning. The usual light that shimmers in Sam's eyes has dimmed, and his shoulders hang heavy, as if he carries bags of sand in each hand.

"About a year," Jess offers, looking between them.

I've been watching Catie since Jess announced who she is, but she's hardly blinked or made any expression to show disappointment or annoyance.

"Nice to meet you." Catie half smiles, reaching out her hand. "I'm Catie Bloom, and this is Sam Harding, my..." Her voice trails off.

"Husband," I finish.

"Nice to meet you both. Thank you for hosting Max. I can already tell this break and reconnection to his life has put a little color into his cheeks." Looking between Max and Jess, I see a thousand unspoken moments and words pass between them, something that only happens when two people have known each other in intimate ways.

"We should leave you two alone." I'm eager to leave, a lump rising in my throat, making it hard to speak or think clearly.

"No," Jess insists. "The sun's coming up, and either you've all had a big night or are about to have a big morning."

"A little of both." Catie forces a laugh. "Would you like to shower? I know how it is after a long day of traveling."

"Thanks, but there's no time."

"Let me get my bags, and I'll meet you downstairs. Natalie makes a killer breakfast," Max says, glancing at me. When our eyes meet, he offers an apologetic smile, and then gives Jess a light kiss on the cheek before leaving the room.

After he's gone, everyone seems unsure of how to act. Sam's hands are in fists as he stands stiffly next to Catie. Catie is darting her eyes at Sam, who is avoiding her looks, and I'm hurt and confused and exhausted. All I want is to get out of this room and this house and be alone, back in my apartment in the city, so I can leave this weekend behind.

"Was it a fun party?" Jess asks.

"Yes," I offer when no one answers. "I think they got some good shots of Max all dressed up, dancing."

"Dancing? He's usually allergic to the notion."

"The EP can be persuasive." Walking toward the bathroom, Catie doesn't turn around when she says, "I better shower and change before everyone else wakes up. I don't want to shock them with all the late-night revelry. Come on, honey."

With deliberate steps, Sam follows Catie. They look almost comical, a mockery of what they are meant to be—a happily married couple living the perfect life.

"Can I fix you something to eat?" I ask, ushering Jess out of the master suite toward the staircase.

"I just need to sit for a minute."

In the living room, Jess walks past the formal sitting area to the sofa in front of the fireplace. I sit next to her on the plush sofa, swallowed by the cushions, and I nestle into their cocoon.

"This townhouse really is beautiful." Jess gingerly sits on the other end of the sofa, her back ramrod straight, reminding me of Max. "I've been a big fan of Mrs. Bloom for a long time. Not that I look it." Jess indicates her loose jeans and pilled green sweater.

"You look lovely."

"I look awful." Jess's face falls into her hands, and her composure crumples.

"I don't look much better." I laugh weakly, but when Jess looks up, her face is still contorted. "What's wrong?"

"I hate to hurt him."

"What do you mean?"

"Max has been through so much, and I don't want to pile more on, but it's better to do this now rather than later, when it's really too late. That's what I keep telling myself."

"What's too late?" I encourage, not daring to get my hopes up.

"No one understands what Max has been through better than me because I went through a lot of it with him. Max was covering my squadron on my second tour in Afghanistan when a suicide bomber attacked a café, killing one of our men. A friend. We were so devastated; everyone in my unit was. But as everyone else gradually dealt with the loss, Max and I clung together, getting sucked up in the grief." Jess rubs her eyes, suddenly looking more tired. "In the middle of our anguish, we got engaged. It wasn't roses and diamonds; it was death and desperation. Max couldn't take it. He went back to travel writing and kept to safer countries like Italy and Spain. It didn't take long for me to realize we'd made a mistake, but then he got hurt and lost his memory. And suddenly, his story was scooped up by the media—thanks to Gillian, I'm sure—and he's been on a whirlwind media tour for the past month.

"Seeing him now, I thought he'd be a mess, but he looks good. Full of life. He may still be in shock, or he may be used to dealing with tragedy by now. Either way, I have to tell him that…that I've met someone. Another man from my unit. And…" Jess stops, taking in her surroundings again. "Am I a horrible person?"

"No. It would be horrible to stay with Max out of obligation or pity. You're doing the right thing." My knee is bouncing, and I stop it with my hand. "Are you hungry? You must be. I'll whip up some omelets and pancakes."

My thoughts are swinging back and forth like a pendulum. Max will be single. But that doesn't mean he's available to me. He's damaged goods. Like, really damaged. Maybe I can patch him back together. Oh, God, how can I be so naïve? He needs a lot of help. More than I could give. I didn't realize that he'd been in an attack in Afghanistan on top of everything else. That's why he was so upset earlier. We all must really look like silly fools to him. And even if he did overlook all the petty drama, who says Max would want me? His eyes have been on my sister from the moment he walked through the door. I have to stop this daydream, this stupid, idiotic, misguided daydream.

In a few minutes, he's going to have his heart broken, and an hour after that, he'll be walking out the door and out of my life for good.

Chapter 18
CATIE

The announcement of Max's engagement was a surprise. But I was more surprised when I didn't feel jealous or disappointed. Instead, I felt nothing. I was still reeling from the nocturnal activities of Sam and Natalie. It was Natalie who looked devastated by Max's news. Could she have a crush on him? I've been so caught up in my own circumstances that I didn't even notice. I am a horrible sister. And I've been chasing after something I don't even want.

Back in the room, Sam ignores me as I move around, collecting my belongings to pack, which are strewn around every corner of the large space. I thought he'd be bursting with smug comments, reveling in the news that Max has been engaged this whole time. But he's quiet, keeping clear of me. It's evident that we've passed the point of no return. Next week, when we're both back at work, he won't find excuses to come to my office or take me out to lunch. I'll hardly see him.

I didn't realize how much I looked forward to his silly texts and our flirty interactions. They'd been fun and innocent—or so I'd thought—and brightened my days. A dark cloud now looms over my future workdays. I can already feel the void his absence will bring. Of course, this all depends on talking our way out of Gillian's idea to make us the new "it" couple without losing our jobs.

My suitcase is open on the floor, clothes spilling out. Packing is too overwhelming. I pull out a pair of shredded white jeans and a blue cashmere sweater, but before I can change out of my gown, the beeping of a van backing into a spot in front of the townhouse draws me to the window. It's the van that delivered the greyhound. "The shelter is here to pick up the dog."

"You better deal with him." Sam shuts the bathroom doors, and the lock clicks.

Outside, a man double the size of the kid who dropped off the dog is taking a drag from a rolled cigarette, his large arms held tight against his body. It's a cold morning, the early sun not up long enough to take the bite out of the air.

"Morning," I say, hugging my bare arms, my gown affording me little warmth.

The man blows smoke above my head in lieu of an answer.

"Sorry you had to get up so early on a Sunday."

He drops his cigarette into the gray slush at his feet; smoke rises around his torn black sneakers until the watery sludge drowns the burning butt. "For three hundred bucks, nothing is too early." He smiles, large gums eclipsing his nubby teeth.

"That seems high. I thought he was a foster dog."

"The money isn't for the dog; it's for the drive to and from Connecticut."

Wow, Gillian really went to a lot of effort to pull the wool over Max's eyes.

"We're one of the few greyhound shelters in the surrounding area. The woman on the phone was insistent that you needed a greyhound for the weekend, and she was willing to pay, so we were willing to drive back and forth." The man's bulbous nose has turned red, likening him to Santa and Rudolph combined. "I'm freezing my nuts off here. Can you get the dog?"

"Right, sorry. I'll go grab him."

In the kitchen, I find Bailey eating from a bowl of fresh food. I wait for him to finish and then clip on his leash and walk him to the man with the van. After he leaves, I walk back into the house and out to the back patio, wanting a moment of peace. I stand at the top of the steps that lead down into the garden and look at my surroundings. I'm in awe of the landscape, illuminated by the morning sun, and I'm in awe of all that Sam has done for me.

The icy air tightens my lungs. *How did I not see what a good man he is?* Because he was too proud. He let me believe that he was a narcissistic womanizer, which also kept him safe. And I wanted to believe it. A man that good looking and confident has to be a heartbreaker. That's what I kept telling myself. And I had the proof. He broke my cousin's heart.

Why do I want him now when I can't have him? And why does it have to hurt so badly? The pressure in my chest pushes upward into my throat, making me all emotional and frustrated and pissed off.

"Dammit!" There's a pile of snow in front of me and I kick it, my foot hitting a frozen chew toy. "Ouch!"

"Are you okay?"

The deep voice startles me. Charles sits forward in one of the patio chairs. My toe aches, and I hobble next to him, falling into the matching chair. White, steamy air surrounds my face as I breathe out heavily, waiting for the pain to subside.

"Anything broken?" he asks, still perched on his chair.

I wiggle my toes. They're sore, but there's no sharp pain. "I don't think so."

"You should put some ice on it."

"They're already numb."

Shrugging out of his oversized black wool coat, he drapes it over my shoulders.

"Oh, thanks." For the first time ever, I take a good look at this man. He's in his midfifties, with a thick head of black hair, which is just starting to recede. His stomach pushes against his slacks, but his broad shoulders and strong arms suggest he was once fit. His face is soft and kind. I'd always seen him as a suit—a man with more power than me—telling me what to do. But right now, he just looks like a man.

"I was surprised to find out Gillian and you are married." I'm not sure why I say it. Yes, I do. From the moment I found out they're married, something has seemed off, and I want to know what it is.

"Technically."

"What does that mean?"

"I shouldn't say anything, but it's not really any big secret. Anyone who knows us knows we've been separated for years."

"Oh," I say awkwardly. I thought there was trouble in their warped paradise, but I didn't expect they were actually living separate lives. "I'm sorry?"

"I'm not." Charles laughs, stretching his legs in front of him. "I miss having my daughter around, but she's in those teenage years, and I'm a little scared of her."

A laugh pops out of my lips. He smiles at me.

"Actually, living with her mom is more practical since I work such crazy hours. I didn't always, but when work is all you have, it's all you do. Going home to an empty apartment is lonely." He stands and walks to the railing, looking out over the white-dusted garden painted pink by the morning sun. "It would be amazing waking up to this every morning. You and Sam should consider moving out to a place like this. Or even better, move to a house in the country. I can see the tension between you two. Getting out of the craziness of the city might help."

"Sam isn't my husband, Mr. Friedman." I'm not sure what makes me confess. Perhaps Charles's own confession. Or exhaustion. Or maybe something bigger. "I've been lying to you. To everyone."

Still gazing out at the small-but-tranquil garden, he draws in a long breath. "First, call me Charles. Second, my own marriage is a sham. And third, everything I do in this business is a lie."

"Not like this. I…" Here it goes. "I don't have a husband, I'm a total slob, and I…I can't cook. I burn toast."

Charles turns, a small smile on his lips. "I don't care. I sell shit for a living. Pretty, tied in a neat bow, BS. And the moment you click off the TV, the BS is gone until tomorrow when I create more BS for the viewers to indulge in and tweet about and blog about. It shouldn't come as a surprise that, in the business of morning TV, none of it would exist without a good helping of crap."

How silly of me to think my lies mattered. At least, to this man. "If only Gillian would see it that way."

"She won't. She has a lot more pride than me and a lot more riding on your name than I do. I can see this weighs heavily on you, and you shouldn't have lied, but don't do anything stupid, like go confessing to all your fans. At least, not without telling me. I may not have integrity, but I know what sells, and I'd like to continue using you on the show. You're good for the ratings."

He turns around, opening the back door, its hinges squeaking.

"What about the reality show Gillian talked to you about? With Sam and me?"

Charles holds the door open with his heel. "There was never a reality show. I told her you guys could come on and do some DIY segments. If Gillian wants a reality show, she'll have to sell it to HGTV or TLC."

"Charles, wait." I slide his coat off and drape it over his arm. "Thank you."

After a few moments enjoying the silence and the relief that at least one person is okay with the truth, I walk inside to the kitchen. David is sitting at the breakfast nook, shoveling eggs into his mouth. Karen is perched on the table next to him, flicking through her iPad, and Charles is ignoring the commotion, listening to the conversation on his phone. Several black equipment bags are beside the table.

"Did you guys spend the night?" I ask, surprised to see them all. The shoot is wrapped.

"We were going over the footage in the dining room all night, grabbing catnaps while we could, in case we needed to take some pick-up shots this morning." Karen takes in my gown. "Where have you been all night?"

"Where do you think?" Gillian jumps in, walking into the kitchen from the back stairs. "She was preparing for the interview."

"We shot the interview last night. You were there," David says, a little smile crossing his lips. He's enjoying the mayhem.

"For...for another interview. She had a lot to prepare." Gillian's cheeks are red, and her eyes are avoiding looking at David. Lies obviously don't come as easily for her. "For the magazine!"

"Relax," I say, leaning across the kitchen counter to the coffee pot and pouring a large cup. "You'll make yourself sick, Ms. Kennedy."

"The van's ready," Charles announces, giving Gillian a quick kiss on the cheek good-bye and telling her he'll see her at home. Then he turns to me and winks. Karen and David pick up the bags around the table and walk outside to load the van. "We've sent the footage from this weekend to the studio, and the special will air at the beginning of next week," Charles says. "I look forward to working with you again soon, Catie. Good luck."

As Charles swings out of the kitchen, Max enters, dropping his luggage next to the island where Jess sits, a large plate of food in front of her. Natalie is at the sink, washing out a pan awkwardly with her good arm, but her eyes are on the action.

"Where have you been all night, Ms. Bloom?" Gillian demands but barrels on before I can answer. "I hope you haven't put the reputation of this magazine in danger."

"Stop trying to control me," I shoot back, feeling bold after my conversation with Charles, and maybe a little delirious from lack of sleep. How can she stand there and give me grief when she is living her own charade. "Don't worry. Nothing happened. Your precious magazine's reputation is still intact."

Gillian's eyes blink rapidly, and her breathing quickens to a racing metronome. I worry she'll have a nervous breakdown right in front of me. "It doesn't matter if nothing happened. It matters what people think happened. Lies can ruin a reputation faster than truth."

Tell me about it.

Max places a hand on her back. "Be careful. Or you'll pass out, Aunt Gilli."

"I saw you! Both of you came back at dawn this morning." Gillian points a slender finger between Max and me. "What if someone else saw you?"

"No one saw us," I say. "What if someone saw you and Charles going home to separate apartments every night."

"What?! What are you talking about? What did he say?" Gillian sputters, blood rushing quickly into her face.

"Ms. Kennedy, you need to relax. You're turning purple," Natalie says, turning off the water and wiping her left hand on her pants to dry it.

"My life has nothing to do with this. It's about you. Your husband. And your image for my magazine. Your readers count on you and your features and blogs and everything they stand for. They want to read about a happy home, easily and effortlessly put together by a faithful wife. They do not want to read about a meandering woman who has affairs and can't keep her family together. I will not have my name dragged through the media mud."

This woman is exhausting. This whole charade is exhausting. I can't do it anymore. She's such a hypocrite. And these lies have pushed the most important people in my life away from me.

"It would be impossible for me to have an affair. I'm not married." The words are out of my mouth before the implication of what I'm doing can hit me. "Not really."

"What? How can that be?" Gillian is storming around the kitchen. Max and Jess lean eagerly over the counter listening.

"Catie didn't mean to lie," Natalie chimes in, but I shoot her a look, and she clamps her mouth shut.

"Everything I write is true. The decorating and household tips, the recipes, even the marriage advice," I explain. "I didn't mean to mislead anyone, but the truth is…Sam and I aren't married." Gillian's face looks like it's about to explode, and I quickly continue, ready to confess everything. "And I'm a horrible slob."

"And you don't know how to cook," Max pipes in.

"How did you…never mind. The point is, it's all been a lie."

"Ms. Kennedy, we did all this for you," Natalie steps in. "For your magazine."

"What if this gets out?" Gillian isn't looking at me, she's pacing the floor, her head down in concentration. "No. No. You didn't do this for me. You've put thousands of people's jobs, their lives, in jeopardy. Everything that is published from any of my press outlets would be scrutinized, ridiculed. It could ruin me!" She looks directly at me. "You're fired."

Chapter 19
CATIE

My body tingles from the adrenaline rushing through it in the aftermath of confessing the truth, but it hasn't sunk in that I no longer have a job. Or an income. Or a chance in hell that Sam will ever forgive me. What does sink to the pit of my belly is that I have to find Sam and break the news that the charade is over and his promotion most likely is too. Imagining his features twisted in anger prevents me from moving from the kitchen. Ruining his life hurts worse than destroying my own.

I take my phone, take a deep breath, and make the first cut, hoping the next one—

when I tell Sam—won't be as painful. I text Patrick.

It's over. Gillian knows.

Nooooooooooooooooooooooooooooooooooooooooooooooooooooooooooooooo ooooooooooooooooooooooooooooooooooooooooooooooooooooooooooooooooooo ooooooooooooooooooooooooooooooooooooooooooooooooooooooooooooooooooo ooooooooooooooooooooooooooooooooooo

This goes on for another thousand characters.

She doesn't know you were involved in the charade. I try and reassure him.

Yet, he replies.

I have no good response because Patrick's probably right. Gillian will figure out pretty fast that my editor would have to have known the truth. My phone rings, but I hit ignore. I have nothing else I can say right now that would reassure Patrick, so I leave it and hope we're wrong, and he keeps his job. He's been at the magazine longer than me, and he's an amazing editor.

Max sits at the table across from me. Natalie and Jess have gone to find Natalie's phone to order a taxi, and the kitchen is so quiet that my ears ring from the lack of noise. We've been sitting across from each other for two minutes, and neither of us has spoken.

"You're engaged," I finally say.

"You're not married," he responds.

"I didn't mean to drag you into this mess. I tried to get out of it, but you see how hard it is to talk to Gillian. She practically bullied me into it." Max raises an eyebrow. "Not that I don't take responsibility. I could have told her the truth as soon as she asked me to do this segment with you."

"Don't sweat it." Max scoots his chair out and walks to the fridge. "This is the most fun I've had in a long time."

As he bends over searching for food, I remember something he said.

"How did you know I couldn't cook?" I raise my cheek from my hand.

The plate of leftover turkey he pulls out is piled high with meat, the sixteen-pound turkey only partially eaten during yesterday's filming. A thick leg hangs out of Max's mouth as he bites down, looking boyish in the jeans and gray sweater he wears. "For starters, you were only in the kitchen during filming. Almost all the prep work was done by Natalie. And when you did accompany her in the kitchen the other night, it was obvious she was the professional. Then I looked up some of your video blogs, and you never actually cook in them. You mix premade ingredients together or stick something in the oven, but I barely saw you chop or do more than sauté some vegetables. When any real cooking or chopping was done, it was in close-up, so all you can see are the hands and arms, and they belonged to Natalie."

"How could you tell?"

"I just could."

I shake my head, smiling. We use a lot of camera and editing tricks in the video blogs, but it wouldn't take much to see through the fog and lights if you were looking. Natalie's nails are short and neat with no polish and her fingers lightly scarred from burns from spending her life in front of burners and ovens. My nails are always long, manicured, and polished. It was a battle to persuade Natalie to put a light-pink polish on her nails any time we filmed. "You're very observant."

"You forget I'm a journalist. But it wasn't that hard to see through the farce. You did try and take a pan out of the oven without an oven mitt."

"I was under a lot of stress!" But I laugh. "I guess a pro knows how to work under pressure."

Standing, I give Max a kiss on the cheek. We've only flirted and almost kissed, but after last night, it's clear we'll only ever be friends. If that. Who knows if I'll see him again after this weekend. "Jess is a lucky girl."

The stripped turkey leg still in Max's hand becomes fascinating to him, reminding me of my dismissive behavior when a fan recognizes me and starts asking me about my husband or a problem with a recipe she's recently tried to make. "She is," Max finally says, his lips not quite making a smile.

The turkey leg is tossed into the trashcan, making it turn on its side from the force. In two steps, Max is beside me. "I need to apologize. Even though you were never married, I shouldn't have...you know. My life has been stalled in some sort of purgatory and being here and flirting with you was a nice distraction. It made me feel alive. Jess is a wonderful woman but she...we both come with a lot of baggage and haunted memories. It was nice to escape all that for a weekend." His arms pull me into a tight hug, my breasts painfully squishing into his chest. "Thank you."

The tears that threaten to spill out make me hold tighter to Max until I feel them slipping back behind my lids. With a big breath, I step back and smile. "And you just made the whole crazy weekend worthwhile. I forgot why I got into this whole business. Funnily enough, it was to help people."

"That's not funny. It's sweet."

"That's not an adjective used to describe me much."

"You're fierce and funny when you don't mean to be, and now you have one more fan."

"Stop. I can't take anymore. I'm not that nice." I sigh. "And now it's time to face up to everything that's happened. I have to find Sam and tell him the bad news."

Halfway up the stairs, I pause, the weight of my situation hitting me. A week ago, I was happily flirting with Sam in my office, not thinking anything of it but loving it all the same. I was in control of my life, moving up: featured on a national TV network, signing the papers on my first home, and a major success in every way in my career. And then the little lies that turned into bigger lies caught up with me.

When I was about seven years old, I stole a cat-shaped pencil sharpener from a neighbor's kitchen counter. As we drove away, I pulled the little object out and showed it to my mom, telling her it had magically appeared in my pocket. Immediately seeing through my lie, she demanded to know where it had come from. Too embarrassed to tell her the truth and face the neighbors, I told her I took it from my dance studio, which had lots of little figurines and trinkets on shelves around the studio. I thought she'd drop it, but she drove the car straight to the studio and made me give it back to Ms. Taul, my ballet teacher. As I approached the teacher, my cheeks burned. Trapped by the situation I'd created, I whispered in her ear that I'd brought her a present and slipped it into her hands, running out of the studio and into the hot car. My mother came out a few minutes later and never said another word. I was too humiliated to ever face Ms. Taul or the studio again, so I quit dancing altogether. Dance was never a great passion of mine, but those little lies, one on top of another, had fallen hard on my small shoulders, making the consequences far worse than they would have been had I first confessed.

And I've done it again…but so much worse. Do we really learn from our mistakes? History seems to repeat itself. These lies have built on one another until they came tumbling down into a rubble of consequences, and this time I'm not the only victim. I've taken Sam and Patrick and Natalie down with me.

I knock lightly on the door of the master bedroom and push it open. Sam's suitcase is packed and sits at the end of the bed. He's standing next to one of the tall windows, reading a piece of paper. I've heard that you can want someone so much that to look at them hurts, and right now, staring at Sam's face, strong and angular, his lips held firmly together in concentration, his dark hair spilling onto his forehead, my insides twist until I feel sick from desire. It's been years since I've had feelings like these, and I hate it. These emotions infect me, spiraling me out of control. I hate being out of control.

My eyes catch sight of the rumpled sheets on the bed, and the image of Natalie wrapped up in Sam's arms accosts me. *Do not look back. Move forward. Take control.* These familiar thoughts run through my head—an old mantra I used to survive the storm of emotions that almost took me under when things with Chris tore my life apart.

Folding the paper he'd been reading, Sam places it in his back pocket and turns, staring at me, an unreadable expression on his face. As he continues to stand before me, not speaking, the silence crushes me more than words could.

"Did you sleep with him?" he finally asks.

"What were you just reading?"

"Nothing. Answer the question."

I glance at my open suitcase and see the letter is missing. A cold tingle assaults my body. It's not anger, though I should be furious at Sam for reading something so personal, but from the realization that if he'd invade my personal property, he really must not care about me or what I'd think if I found him with the letter. He didn't try to hide it when I came in. The tingles spread, and I break out in a cold sweat. He really doesn't love me. My actions this weekend have stripped him of any love he once felt for me.

"Does it matter?" I say, in answer to his question. I wish I could drop my guard and be real with Sam, but pushing him away is easier than dealing with the consequences of him knowing that I've fallen for him. I fell for him a long time ago. But what does it matter when he's not in love with me anymore.

Too little, too late.

His long fingers strangle the back of the sofa he leans back on. "It might to his fiancé."

"Then let her worry about what Max and I did or didn't do." The underside of my arms burns, raw from rubbing against the sequins of my dress all night. Taking the blue cashmere sweater and white jeans I picked out earlier, I walk into the bathroom, needing to unburden myself of the heavy gown.

"You don't care that he's engaged?" Sam yells from the bedroom.

"Don't act all self righteous," I toss back through the open door, unzipping the side zipper of my dress. "You were the one making out with your *wife's* sister."

"Behind closed doors and you're not my wife."

"Thank God," I mumble, letting the dress fall to the ground in a heap. I hear the door to the bedroom click open. Sam is leaving. I can't stall any longer.

"Gillian fired me."

There's silence, and I think Sam has already left, which means I'll have to run after him, and all I'm wearing are my strapless bra and lacey black underwear. Before I can take a step, a movement in the mirror startles me. Sam stands just inside the bathroom, staring at me. Well, at my breasts. I've never been shy about my figure, but my whole body tightens into a ball of insecurity as he stares. I'd reach for a towel, but I don't want him to know that I care.

"It's just underwear."

"I'm not…I wasn't…it just took me by surprise." He rakes his eyes back to my face and his jaw tightens, the muscle twitching behind his cheek.

"You won't be getting that promotion." *Why am I being such a bitch?* I know why. It's called self-preservation, and I'm a master at it.

Panic flashes across his eyes before they narrow, and his hand flicks out, grabbing my arm, and for the first time in my life, I'm turned on by a man being rough with me. It goes against every feminist urge in my body, but I can't help it. It's hot. His face is so serious, and if I had more courage, I'd lay one on him.

"Why?" The one word squeezes out from his clinched jaw.

"It was time to tell her the truth." I grimace as his hand tightens.

Seeing my expression, he quickly drops his hand, but his eyes bore into mine, trying to read my thoughts. "Did you do it to punish me?"

"No! Geez, Sam. I might be selfish, but I'm not hateful."

"Why did you do it?"

"Because I found out that Gillian's own marriage is a sham. Charles and her have been separated for years. And because of what you said about me using people. I don't want to lie anymore."

Looking around him, Sam seems to focus on a thought. "That's nice that you've suddenly grown a conscience, but you took the whole ship down with you. Patrick will be fired. I won't get the promotion, and I'll most likely be fired. Why ruin it for everyone after everything we've done for you? Were you trying to act noble for Max, so you could win him back on your own terms?"

"It had nothing to do with him!" I take a moment to compose myself, which isn't easy since I'm still in my underwear. "You say I'm selfish for not telling Gillian. Now I'm selfish for telling Gillian. I can't win with you, Sam."

"Telling Gillian was one of the most selfish things you've ever done." Sam throws a balled up towel at me, and I flinch. It falls to my feet, but I snatch it up, wrapping it around my body. "I knew you weren't perfect. It was your flaws that made me fall for you. Now I can't believe I ever loved you."

Reaching into his back pocket, he tosses the piece of paper he'd been reading earlier at my feet. He's gone, and one word reverberates in my ears with the sound of the slamming door.

Loved.

A few stunned moments pass before I register the piece of paper. Picking it up, I see that I was right. It's the letter I never opened from Chris. I open it; the familiar writing instantly makes my heart clamp tight inside my chest, afraid of what I'm about to read.

Dear Kit-Cat,

I pause, sucking back emotion as I see my college nickname, so foreign and familiar all at once.

> *I know it's antiquated to write a letter these days, but I didn't want you to receive the divorce papers without an explanation from me.*
>
> *First, I know I'm a decade too late, but I need to apologize. I'm sorry. You were, and I'm sure still are, an amazing, loving, fun, generous woman. I've never forgotten how you dropped everything—paused your whole life—to be with me when my mother was sick. It's the most unselfish thing anyone has ever done for me.*
>
> *I was a mess after we returned to school that fall. My mother was on the mend, but almost losing her terrified me, and I let the fear fester inside me. Seeing her so close to death shook me to the core. I shut down and pushed everything I loved away, including you. I did love you, Catie. I'm sorry I was so cruel. I don't even remember half of the things I did or said that year, but I know they were awful. It's not an excuse, but I hope an explanation might help you understand and forgive me.*
>
> *We were so young.*
>
> *I've watched your career soar over the years, and I want to brag to everyone that I am married to that incredible woman. But I don't. It's not my glory to take.*
>
> *As you may have guessed from these papers, I'm getting married, again. She's a kind and generous woman, and you'll probably never meet her, but I think you would really like her.*

*Please forgive me. I've only ever wanted
the best for you.*

*With Love,
Christophe*

*P.S. Since we never got a divorce, I've
always wondered how you married again. In any
case, I hope he loves you fiercely, passionately, and
generously. It's the only way to love and be loved.*

As I read the last line, I let the tears slip out. We *were* so young. I knew the near death of his mother scared him, but I never guessed how much. When I lost my father, I was a kid. I was sad, but I didn't really understand it. When Chris's mom recovered, I just assumed we'd go back to the way things were. But even from that point on, Chris had us on some rollercoaster romance—moving in, getting married. He needed the visa, but it was more than that. He wanted the security of marriage. He'd almost lost his family. But once the initial shock wore off, he must have regretted the marriage and blamed me. It's no wonder he lashed out. It's not right, but all the pieces are clicking together.

For the first time, I realize I wasn't a fool. It was a complicated and crazy situation that I was too young and naïve to understand until now. The tears keep coming, washing away the guilt and fear and foolishness I've felt for so many years. When all that's left in me are dry hiccups, I sit up and take a soul-cleansing breath.

The tears washed away the claustrophobic emotions that have held me back for years, and I suddenly feel empowered.

No job? No problem. No man? No problem. Sometimes you have to lose to win.

Oh, God, did I just think that?

There are no winners here this weekend. Only losers, and I am the biggest loser of all. So I guess that does make me a winner. A very pathetic winner of losers.

I'll get back on top. I always do. I have to. Except, right now I don't have the energy to believe it just yet. The emotional purge and lack of sleep take over, and I fall into bed, closing my eyes. I see Sam behind my eyelids, and I want to wrap my arms around him and tell him I'm ready. I can do this. But my heart beats heavily in my chest, knowing that my chance with him is over.

I know in time I'll get over it and find someone else to love. But the only person I want to love right now is Samuel Harding.

Chapter 20

NATALIE

After a shower and fresh clothes, I feel like a new woman. It may have taken a half hour longer than usual, but it's not easy with only one good arm. Now I'm in the kitchen, sliding the leftover French toast into a Tupperware container. Jess pours us both a cup of coffee. I was about to keel over after breakfast from exhaustion, but the shower has revived me.

Gillian is hovering near the counter, eyeing the leftovers, as I snap the lid onto the Tupperware container, but I refuse to offer her a morsel, and she doesn't ask. Though her stomach has gurgled loudly. Twice.

Her phone pings. "My car's here," she says, picking up her Louis Vuitton duffel, giving the French toast one last look before leaving.

Heavy steps on the back staircase reveal Sam, a scowl etched on his face.

"Have you seen Gillian?"

I lift a dirty spatula I'm placing in the sink, pointing in the direction of the front door. Sam hurries out of the kitchen after her.

"He looks pissed." The plate Jess holds under the running faucet tips sideways, water spraying over the counter. "Shoot. Sorry about that."

I take the plate from Jess and place it on the counter, drying it the best I can with one hand. Keeping my voice neutral, I ask the question that's been running through my head since Jess walked into the kitchen. "Have you talked to Max yet?"

"I'm avoiding it. I need to tell him soon. Now. The plane we're about to board is taking us to our friend's cabin in Vail, and Mark, that's my"—Jess does a quick check that no one has entered the kitchen unannounced—"boyfriend, will be there. I have no idea how Max is going to react."

As Jess piles the cleaned dishes on the counter, I take a dish towel and continue to wipe it over them. "Shouldn't he have more than a few minutes to decide if he's going to spend a week with the girl who's just dumped him and her new lover?"

The startled look on Jess's face makes me almost regret my bluntness, but after a weekend of lies, I've lost my patience.

"I better go find him." Jess smiles weakly and leaves the room.

"If this is about the editor position—" Gillian's voice blasts as she swings back into the kitchen.

Sam tears in after Gillian. "It's about Catie and—"

"She's fired." Gillian opens the fridge and pours a glass of orange juice. "I need food. My blood sugar is too low." Gillian piles French toast onto a plate, but I snatch it out of her hands, dumping it in the sink with a clatter. Gillian looks as if I've slapped her. My heart gallops in my chest. I can't believe I did that. "What the hell do you think you're doing? I'll—"

"Fire me? Like you fired my sister?"

Gillian waves her hand, dismissing my outburst. "I didn't make her lie to me or her readers."

I point the spoon I'm drying at her. "You were the one who went on and on about how important this special was. How great it would be for the profile of the magazine and your publication. She did everything she could to get out of it, to tell you no, but you wouldn't listen to her."

Sam pops the lid off the Tupperware container and dishes out two more pieces of French toast. He sits at the table, smiling at the back-and-forth between Gillian and me. I'm surprised he finds this amusing. This may be the end of his career too.

"It doesn't matter anymore," Sam says, dousing his French toast with maple syrup. "I've been trying to tell you that Charles told Catie this morning that she's good for ratings and has offered her a permanent position on their morning show."

Oh no! Catie can't take that job without continuing the charade. I thought this was finally over.

"How can he even consider hiring her now that I've fired her?" Gillian asks, crossing her arms.

Sam glances at me and widens his eyes at me, trying to convey a message. *Is he lying? Does he need help?* I quickly take over, hoping I'm reading his clues correctly.

"Sam's right. I heard Charles talking to Catie," I say, and when Sam doesn't stop me, I continue. "I'm surprised he didn't tell you. You two are married, aren't you?" I hold back a smile at my own dig.

"Charles was really impressed with Catie this weekend," Sam says, shoving a piece of toast in his mouth, chewing. "And the network wants to snatch her up before another network snags her first. So Catie doesn't need you or your magazine."

"I've been begging Charles to take one of my people on for years. Of course, he offers the job to the one person I've just fired," Gillian bursts out. "Unless…" I can almost see the wheels inside Gillian's head spinning, worried she made a mistake firing Catie.

"I'm not sure Catie will want to come back." Sam swallows his last bite and leans back, his voice measured. "You better go tell her now and make it official."

Gillian exhales loudly and then stomps up the stairs.

"Was that true?" I ask Sam.

"For the most part."

Picking up my phone, I text Catie and tell her to go along with anything Gillian says about an offer from Charles.

"Something smells amazing," Max says, walking into the kitchen. My breath catches at the sight of him, looking relaxed and strong as he flings his duffel bag on the ground.

"Where's Jess?" Sam asks, making a plate for Max.

"On her way to the subway." Max gulps down a cup of coffee and pours a second

"Why aren't you with her?"

"She dumped me." Max flashes a bright smile, as if he's announced he's engaged, not disengaged.

"What?" Sam and I bust out.

How can Max be happy about this? I wonder.

"She's with another man from her unit. I know him. Great guy." Max bites into a piece of French toast. "She's off to meet up with him."

"Aren't you upset?"

"I'm more upset I won't be going skiing in Colorado. I could still go, but it might be a bit awkward." Seeing the disbelieving looks on our faces, he explains. "I'm not that surprised. We both knew the engagement was a mistake. Our emotions were running high over there, but when you get back to reality, things become clear. If she didn't do it first, I would have."

Sam's shoulders hunch. "Catie will be happy. You should go upstairs and tell her the news."

"She knows." Max wipes his mouth and sits back, looking at Sam. His expression is a mix of glee and self-satisfaction. "But I'm not interested in women who are in love with someone else."

"What do you mean?" Sam sits back, matching Max's calm exterior, but his hands are clutched at his sides as he waits for Max to answer.

"Catie is in love with you, man." Max smiles knowingly.

"She doesn't love me. I hate to break the news, but we're not married."

"I know. I was here when she confessed everything to Gillian. It was really brave."

I slide closer, wondering where Max is going with this conversation. I also thought Max would be running up the stairs to confess his feelings to Catie.

"She was confused at first, but last night she admitted it," Max continues. "I think it was the first time she admitted it even to herself. She is one hundred percent in love with you."

Sam pushes his chair back. "Excuse me."

After he leaves, I turn to Max. "Is that true?"

"Yes. The only way a man can get under a woman's skin like that is if she loves him." Max wipes his mouth, grabbing his duffel bag. "I better get going."

"Where to?"

"I don't know." His eyebrows rise at the realization, and he laughs. "I'm actually really bummed not to be going skiing. This guy's cabin is unreal. It sleeps like twenty people, and you ski right out the back door."

"That does sound amazing. I've never been skiing, but it's on my bucket list."

"How about this—I'll take you skiing as soon as your arm is healed."

I laugh. "I'd rather go to a tropical island. I'm sick of all this cold and drear."

"Seriously, we should get you that X-ray. Maybe after that, you can take me to the best hot chocolate in New York City. It's not a tropical island, but it'll warm our insides."

"I make the best hot chocolate in the city." I beam.

"Done." Max smiles and then looks around the kitchen. "What happened to Bailey?"

"The shelter came and picked him up. We were just fostering him for the weekend."

Max slings the bag over his shoulder. "Then I need to go see a man about a dog."

My eyes widen. "Oh, you mean go to the shelter. It's in Connecticut."

"Can you drive me?"

"I don't have a car." Then my eyes fall to the muscles that are dancing in his arm as he moves his bag from hand to hand, and something grips me deep inside. I'd be a fool to refuse. "Okay—give me a few minutes to pack, and we can get a taxi." I start laughing. This is miles from where I thought I'd end up at the end of this weekend.

"What's funny?"

"An hour ago, I thought you'd be running after Catie as soon as you found out she wasn't married and now..." I leave the statement unfinished, not wanting to assume anything and not ready to put my heart out there for Max to reject quite yet.

"Why would I want her?" Max winks. "She doesn't know how cook."

Chapter 21

CATIE

"What do you want?"

Gillian has barged into my room, blustering around, but so far she's made no sense. She's talking about raises and bonuses and loyalty. How did she go from firing me to giving me incentives to stay? Natalie's cryptic text isn't helping, but I keep my mouth shut.

"You can't leave the magazine. You have a responsibility to your readers."

"I didn't leave it. You got rid of me." I yawn, sitting up in the bed, trying to get my bearings.

"Good. Then you'll stay on."

"I didn't say that. I already—" I wasn't exactly sure how I was going to finish that statement. With another lie, most likely, but Gillian cuts me off with an incredible statement.

"Sam told me about Charles's job offer at *Wake Up*. But you'll need a place to continue to build your platform. Plus, we made you into the media sensation you are today. We're your family."

"I made me. Your publication helped, and the amazing people who work for you were an incredible support, but you

191

weren't. You're a hypocrite. You talk about truth and integrity, but all weekend you've been nitpicking at me, making sure I fit *your* perfect image of what I should be, and…and what about the dog. Yes! You had your assistant find a doppelgänger for Max's dog that died and tried to pass it off as his own."

"Ms. Bloom. Catie—"

"And your marriage is a lie! Charles told me you've been separated for years," I yell, tired of her bullying. "At the front of every one of your publications is a picture of you and your family and a statement about how you value your magazines as much as your family. It's all a lie."

"No, it's not. We're married."

"Charles doesn't even live with you."

I fling the bathroom doors open and spread toothpaste over my toothbrush. I can't believe the things coming out of my mouth. I feel invigorated and free for the first time in years. Sam has gone above and beyond again. I can't believe he lied—or at least exaggerated the truth—but it has Gillian in a frenzy, and I like the shift in power.

"Of all the self-important, selfish people…if it wasn't for me you'd—"

"Be happy." I push the toothbrush back and forth over my teeth before spitting. "I'll consider coming back, but only if you promise to keep Patrick and Sam." I'd like for Gillian to grovel some more, but I'm not an idiot. I have to salvage their jobs first.

"I wasn't going to fire them." Gillian's face sobers. "I may come across as harsh and unforgiving—you have to be, as a woman in my position—but I've always been fair with my employees. You can't blame me for being upset and even wanting to fire you for your deception. But I don't believe in taking the whole ship down just because of one passenger that's full of you-know-what. Patrick is a great editor. I'd be an idiot to let him go. And I almost admire Samuel Harding for his loyalty to you. If he has as much loyalty for his work, I'll never let him leave."

"Good." Holding back my triumphant smile, I put my hand out. She shakes it, my whole body jiggling at the force until she lets go and tramps out.

Trying to comprehend what just happened, I know I'll be groveling to Sam for a while. It was one of the few lies worth telling this weekend. It would have been sweet revenge to tell Gillian to go stuff it, but I can't. I had to make sure Patrick and Sam kept their jobs. But I no longer feel tied to Gillian or the magazine. After the madness has calmed down, it may be time for me to step away and start something for myself.

My phone buzzes, and I look to see another missed call from Patrick. I shoot him a quick text.

False alarm. All is well. Jobs all still intact.

Immediately, I receive a text back.

I hate you.

I smile, knowing he means the opposite.

The tightness in my chest that has accompanied me since I started this sham of a weekend finally loosens—but there's a different pulling in my gut that won't subside. It would be nice to pretend I don't know why I still feel ill, but I'm too exhausted to lie anymore, even to myself.

Why can't I forget about Sam and his stupid declaration?

Just thinking his name sends flutters of excitement and terror through me. I dump my suitcase on the bed and gather my clothes from around the room.

Why couldn't he have been honest with me from the beginning? But I'm not one to preach honesty. No, sirree. Ugh! He's so damn frustrating! And so panty-dropping hot. I'd hate him if I didn't love him so much.

The fury and frustration explodes to the surface, and I grab a pillow and scream into its plush surface.

At the sound of a creaking floorboard, I drop the pillow and see Sam. He takes deliberate steps toward me, his face covered in a potpourri of emotions. His lips are pressed tightly together, but there's a gleam behind his eyes and a twitch in his jaw that reveals amusement.

"Before you yell at me again, you should know—"

Grabbing my shoulders, Sam presses his lips against mine. My body goes limp, until the fear and anger that have been coursing through my veins stir again, and I push him off.

"What are you doing?" I move backward, my hands up.

"What I've wanted to do to you for the past four years."

Oh, my.

Sam moves toward me, and I keep my arms raised.

"This isn't funny."

"I'm not laughing." Sam's eyes go all dark and serious, and butterflies tackle my stomach. I tell them to cut it out.

"You hate me. You love me. You hate me," I say. "I'm sick of playing games."

"So am I." Sam's hands, strong and sure, reach out for me again.

"Stop."

A car door slams outside, and there's the sound of an engine starting. "Your boyfriend's leaving. Aren't you going to run after him?" Sam is smiling.

I look out the window and watch Max putting his luggage into a taxi with Natalie's luggage. *What is she doing?* I push the window up. "Natalie, wait!"

I turn back to Sam, who looks confused. "Hold that thought," I tell him and run down the stairs and out the front door. I won't be able to concentrate until I speak to Natalie.

"What's the matter? Didn't Gillian give you your job back?" Natalie asks.

"Yes, but I don't want it. I want to work with you." When I was telling Gillian off, in the back of mind I knew it was because I don't want my job back. I've loved working with Natalie all these years, but now I want to do it right.

"What are you talking about?"

"Let's start our own business. We can write another book but this time with both our names on the cover. It'll help promote your restaurant and shop, and I could start my own furniture-design business. I've wanted to for years. And I did have a good talk with Charles right before he left, and I think he'd continue to work with me, even without the magazine. In fact, I think he'd do it just to piss off Gillian. It'll be a lot of work at first, and maybe I'm crazy, but I think we could build this into something. Together."

Natalie stares at me like I have a monkey on my head, but then she breaks into a smile and throws her good arm around me. "Yes! Of course! Let's do it!"

We jump up and down, holding each other, adrenaline pushing out the cold around me. I step back, satisfied, and take in the taxi and Max waiting patiently on the other side.

"Where are you going?"

"To get my arm checked and then to the shelter. Max called, and they're holding the dog for us."

"Us?" I ask, wanting to warn Natalie to tread carefully, but I don't. I'm not one to give advice on love.

"For Max."

The taxi driver honks his horn lightly, and Natalie waves apologetically. "I better go."

"Come over tomorrow, and let's talk about the book and business."

Natalie looks up to the window on the second story. Sam's head is against the pane, watching us.

"I think you're gonna be busy for the next few days. I'll call you next week."

After another hug, I watch them drive away and walk back up to the bedroom. Every step closer sends my heart pounding, until I'm dizzy with anticipation. Seeing Sam when

I walk back into the room makes every part of me freeze, and I halt just inside the door.

"When you ran down there"—Sam takes two deliberate steps toward me—"I thought you were running after Max."

"I told you, it's not like that. I don't love him."

"Who do you love?"

My lips fall silent. I can't tell another lie, but I can't tell the truth. Not when everything I've ever wanted stands in front of me, wrapped in a knee-quivering package. My insides turn sideways at the thought of never touching him, or worse, feeling every part of him and then having him leave me cold and alone. My gut tells me Sam is not that kind of man, but how do I know that until I take the leap?

"You don't have to say it. Max told me."

"Told you what?"

"You're in love with me."

Unable to meet Sam's intense stare, I walk toward the window, the sun almost blinding me as it reflects off the snow. "It doesn't matter."

"It always matters." Sam slides his fingers around my waist, grazing the exposed skin above the waistband of my jeans. Heat pulsates in every direction over my body, up to my chest, making my heart thunder inside my rib cage, and down to my inner thighs, pressure building inside, making it hard to think about anything except his touch. "I'm in love with you."

The words send a shower of emotions over me—joy, terror, desire—and I let out a sigh. Sam slowly caresses the tender skin below my belly button, and the muscles in my legs lose all function, and I fall into him, his hands tightening around my waist. He breathes in deeply at the nape of my neck as the soft pillows of his lips begin to tease the delicate skin. It's the most erotic moment of my life.

"You smell amazing."

"Stop." I push away, still wobbly.

"I won't hurt you."

The sweet words release a whimper from my throat. All the fear, hurt, pain, and heartbreak pour out of me in a stream of silent tears. I hear the truth in his voice. He won't hurt me. He'll love me the way I need to be loved. This man who was always there, but who I never really saw, sees me as I am and loves me.

Dropping all the fight from my body, I let him hold me. The rapid pounding in his chest matches my own heartbeat, and I turn my face. Looking into his eyes, I almost come apart from the love that bursts into every part of me. "I love you too."

I close my eyes, and his hands cup my face. His lips, soft and searching, press into mine. His hands move under my shirt as he traces the skin of my lower back, goose bumps erupting all over my flesh. I moan, my lips popping open as he slides his tongue inside, and I almost pass out from the cacophony of emotions accosting me. If his hands weren't gripping me so tightly, I'd fall into a heap of ecstasy on the floor.

When he pulls back, I look at him in awe and wonder, a smile I've never experienced spreading across my lips. "If you continue to kiss like that, I'll make our little marriage arrangement permanent."

He kisses me again, enveloping me in a blanket of love and desire. "I don't scare that easily."

Our bodies topple to the bed, and we're laughing and kissing and exploring. It's divine. My love for this man is so overpowering it hurts. This amazing man loves me and my many flaws. I could say it was my lies that made him love me, but that might be overstating it a bit. Whatever the reason, he loves me, and finally, I know that I love him.

This is going to be a very good New Year.

COMING SOON

The Adventures of

Natalie Bloom

by
Brooke Stanton

For a sneak peek and other goodies, sign-up for
Brooke's mailing list at her website,
brookestantonbooks.com

ACKNOWLEDGMENTS

As Ernest Hemingway so eloquently wrote, "The first draft of anything is shit." Thank you to everyone who helped me along the way from first draft to last. Thanks to my team of publishing bandits: Julie Miesionczek, Lindsey Nelson, Silvia Curry, and Daliborka Mijailovic. Rachel and Adam Bloom for having such an awesome last name. My best friend and always one of my first readers, Corinne Barlow. To my amazing mom, Sue, who read many versions of this book. To Caroline O'Brien and our team of creative Goddesses. You girls are my biggest cheerleaders. And to my husband, Mick, who made all this possible with your support, love, generosity, and compassion—a Domestic Goddess I am not!

ABOUT THE AUTHOR

After her own misadventures in New York City, LA, and London, **Brooke Stanton** now lives in sunny South Florida. She's an award-winning author who has contributed to *Natural Awakenings Magazine*, wrote a column for *Examiner.com*, and is the author of The Bloom Sisters series. Visit her website at brookestantonbooks.com.

Made in the USA
Lexington, KY
17 July 2016